****

DIPPED IN THE FIRE

****

A Novel by
Bestselling Author

Jeanetta Britt

Inquiries should be addressed to J. Britt
(brittbooks@msn.com)
Twelve Stones Publishing LLC
P. O. Box 921, Eufaula, AL 36072-0921
www.jbrittbooks.com

Library of Congress Control Number: 2016900197
ISBN: 978-0692650646

Printed in the United States
First Edition

Editor: Fairrene Carter-Frost
Glorias G. Dixon
Cover: Michelle Stimpson

Scriptures from *The Holy Bible*
King James Version

To my
Fisk University Family
—past, present, future—
Upon the celebration of our Sesquicentennial (1866-2016)
150 years of committed faith, academic excellence,
and dedicated service to the world community.
"...for the Gold and the Blue..."
Fisk Forever!

Pure Gold

So much in this life
Is intended to set fire to your soul
But Jesus controls the thermostat
And Believers come forth as pure gold.

Acknowledgments

Since writing, for the most part, is such a solitary journey, I'm very grateful for friends who understand and support. Thank you, Glorias Dixon (*Fisk*), for always challenging my ideas and making me leave some stuff on the cutting room floor. Thanks, Fairrene Carter-Frost, for sifting through the remains and making them better. Many thanks to Dr. William Gittens (*TSU*) and his willingness to share his first-hand knowledge of the Nashville experience that we both know and love. Thank you, Britt Stewart, for keeping me up on the latest slangs and cultural trends—always keeping it relevant; always keeping it real. Thanks, Jewel Harris and Sylvia Banks, for your constant support. And what would any book be without a cover that...pops? Michelle Stimpson—National bestselling author, Christian writer, Educator—thank you for another brilliant effort and for having the patience to put up with me and my critical eye.

And for all my wonderful readers who love the Scriptures as I do—on the lines and between the lines—thank you for your amazing reviews and comments that put our faith on display in this contemporary world.

And a big thanks to all my friends and family, who allow me to skip out of the circle for a beat, and then welcome me back with open arms when it's time to jump back in, again. I love you.

ഏ

May the Lord be pleased with our efforts to lift Him up…
for He gives us this awesome privilege
with a precious promise…
(John 12:32)

PROLOGUE
Gold Digger

"Well, Sister Mann…may I call you, Melissa?"

"But of course, Brother Grand…if I may call you, Douglas," Melissa said sweetly, flashing her alluring eyes in his direction. Her deep-set almond eyes were like liquid pools of molten lava, and many a man had plunged into their seductive depths to their own peril.

"Of course you may, Melissa." Douglas smiled to put his perfect white teeth on display. His deep, raspy voice might've seemed harsh to some, but most of the ladies in his circle had labeled it downright sexy. "I'm just glad you agreed to have dinner with me this evening," he said, as the candlelight flickered between them at their corner table for two at Chez Jacques, which boasted of the finest French cuisine Nashville, Tennessee had to offer.

"I'm delighted for the invitation." The color flushed in Melissa's creamy, brown cheeks, and she brushed back a strand of her luxurious, black curls that swept over her shoulders. "After all," she said in her most polished tone, "we do have the first quarter numbers to consider." She was an ambitious, single woman approaching 35, but it was a well-kept secret between her and her birth certificate. And aside from having the face and figure of a runway super model, she had a pair of long, supple legs that got lots of whistles from passersby, followed by one, single word—"Stallion".

"Surely, there's no more important business than church business." Douglas' handsome brown eyes glowed. His deep chocolate face was framed by a head full of black, rippling waves, a well-trimmed moustache and short sideburns, which defied his 38 years. And coupled with his athletic, six-foot frame, he always got lots of attention in his well-tailored suits. He was wearing a charcoal gray one with a gold silk tie and matching square for the occasion.

"Yes, church business is very important," Melissa commented. "And it's amazing to me that True Vine is doing as well as it is considering Pastor Meadows refuses to pass the offering plate, but insists on trusting everyone to drop their tithes and offerings into the box at the door as they exit."

"I've had that conversation with him many times." Douglas admitted. "But he's a man with rock-solid beliefs and strong convictions, and it seems to be working for him and the church so far. We're just blessed to have such a large, affluent congregation...the kind with big bank accounts, who don't mind giving."

"True." Melissa chuckled. "And I suppose strong men attract each other, Douglas." She inserted skillfully. "It has always fascinated me how you can find the time to chair the church's Finance Committee with your booming enterprise and busy schedule." Her cheeks burned as she tried not to appear too eager. "You're becoming a household name in the music industry, right here in Music City USA."

"Well, you find the time to do it, Melissa," Douglas remarked as his chest swelled, "even with all your executive-level responsibilities at the IRS.

"We all have to make sacrifices," Melissa said primly. Although, in actuality, in spite of her MBA and CPA and ten years on the job, she'd only risen to mid-level management at the IRS. But if the church's elite somehow got the notion she was something more than that, based on her over-inflated tithes and offerings, who was she to correct them; right? "But I'm just in an office, Douglas," she said, keeping it soft and sweet, "you're building your own...empire—"

"Yes, but one must always make time for the Lord's work," Douglas quipped.

"Oh, my—" Melissa gasped; his words rumbling through her like a loaded freight train.

"Melissa?" Douglas called her back to the present. "Is something wrong?"

"Oh, no," Melissa said, shifting self-consciously. "That's just something my daddy used to always say. He was a pastor, you know?"

"No, I didn't know." Douglas' brown eyes rounded in amusement. "So you're a *PK*, huh?"

"Pardon?" Melissa stiffened her upper lip. She disliked the term and the dubious distinction it carried. The offspring of clergy were often held to a higher standard of conduct, and sometimes they slid from their lofty perch, only to be branded the worst of the lot.

"A preacher's kid?" Douglas smiled against her obvious reluctance to discuss it.

"Well, yes." Melissa admitted quietly.

"Where's your daddy's church?"

"Faith Freewill of Knoxville," Melissa said, shifting in her chair. "I grew up in Knoxville, you know?"

"No." Douglas leaned in to hear more. "I didn't know. Is he still preaching?"

"No. He's gone." Melissa sniffed bravely. "And I just recently lost my Mother, as well." She confided, very much aware Douglas' eyes were lapping her up like a bowl of warm milk.

"So sorry to hear that," Douglas said, eyes glued to her rounded cleavage. "You have my deepest condolences."

"It was a lovely service," Melissa said demurely. "There were a host of important people in attendance, and flowers came from as far as the White House—"

"White House, huh?" Douglas was duly impressed, and his growing desire for Melissa just cranked up a notch. She obviously had connections with people in high places; a prospect he always found exciting. "Well, my parents are gone, too," he said. "Guess us orphans have to stick close together, huh?"

"Guess so." Melissa's heart fluttered at the gleam in his eye and the double-meaning in his words.

"Siblings?"

"Brother." Melissa zipped pass the topic. She had absolutely no desire to dredge up his unpleasant saga on a special night like this.

"Well, that's one of the few pleasures in life I've missed." Douglas' ego bailed her out, seeing as how every topic seemed to find its way back to him. "No siblings." He shrugged. "So I got my parents' undivided attention, which made me want to run away from home as quickly as possible."

"Well, maybe that's what gave you such drive." Melissa flattered, deflecting her luscious eyes into her lap.

"So you're a PK, huh?" Douglas' fine nostrils flared as he maneuvered the conversation back in his direction. He lived on just this side of ruthless, and he was a man accustomed to manipulating every situation; getting his own way; using all of his assets to his best advantage. "I knew there was something very charming and distinctive about you…in addition to your class and beauty, Melissa." He eyed her admiringly. Even close up, she was the most gorgeous woman he'd ever seen. He liked what she had to offer. So he wanted to play his cards just right and not give her the impression that she was out of his league. "I couldn't help but notice how well-suited you are for your work on the Finance Committee and church work, in general." He teased. "Now, maybe I've stumbled upon your secret. You've been groomed to be a classy lady from birth." He winked, and the seductive smile that followed drew her in like a magnet. "That's why I'm glad you agreed to have dinner with me. I feel there's so much more about you I need to know."

"Oh-h." Melissa giggled, fanning away his compliment with her napkin. "Who in their right mind would turn down an invitation to

Chez Jacques?" She flattered. "You've got to be on Nashville's A-list just to get a reservation."

Douglas smiled proudly and let the moment pass. He sat back satisfied as their appetizer of imported foie gras came and went.

Melissa attempted to spread the rich goose liver pâté onto the delicate cracker like it was something she did every day, but peanut butter and jelly were more her usual fare. She'd spent so much of her modest income to lease a condo in the Brentwood Estates area, south of downtown Nashville—the neighborhood of the rich and famous; the home of True Vine Ministries, Inc., 'mega-church to the stars'— that she had to scrimp somewhere. With her tight budget bursting at the seams, she'd come up with 101 ways to turn Ramen noodles and canned tuna fish into delectable delights. Necessity, yet again, proving to be the mother of invention.

As the main course of beef tenderloin and spring vegetables was served by the white-gloved waiter, Douglas pushed back a little and said, "Melissa, you were wrong earlier." He straightened his imported tie. "My name is not *yet* a household word in the music industry, but it will be when I expand my artist promotion services in New York, L.A., Miami—worldwide—wherever good music is made and played." His eyes blazed. "My *empire*, as you so aptly put it, is on the rise."

"Is that so?" Melissa said, masking her excitement under a sweet smile, but his raw ambition was turning her on. She'd always wanted to be the wife of a rich and powerful man so she could feel safe and significant. That's why she'd groomed herself so meticulously and spent all of her hard-earned dollars to place herself in the right environment to achieve her goal. It was an investment in her success, after all, to get up-close-and-personal with a man like Douglas Grand. And right now, his passion about his work and his future was like music to her ears. *But*— She looked down at the wide, gold wedding band, which was a new addition to his well-manicured left hand. *He's a married man.* She gulped a sip of her sweet tea. *Who knew?*

"Yes, I'm making progress." Douglas' words flowed, thick and rich like spun gold. "But you have some standout qualities of your own, Melissa."

"Me?" Melissa's brows arched perfectly, compliments of her countless hours at the priciest brow bar in the city. She sparkled like the poster-child of surprise; even though, she'd spent the better part of the day and her paycheck getting ready for an evening to remember with this special man. Having just lost her mother in February, she'd hoped this April evening would restart the clock for her in 2013. She'd worn her Vera Wang raw silk ensemble to ward off the cool of a spring night in Nashville. She looked stunning in the color fuchsia, and she knew it. The form-fitting dress offered a stiff whiff of cleavage; her five-inch Versace pumps put her lean, shapely calves on full display; and when her matching cape was whisked off with a flourish, she expected and earned the admiring glances of all the tables of rich patrons in the private dining room.

"Yes, you're quite a beautiful lady, Melissa Mann." Douglas smiled at her like he'd already sealed the deal. "And that's the other reason I invited you here to dine with me tonight."

"Really?" Melissa returned his gaze behind her veil of thick, dark lashes.

"I need…some feminine advice…and you're the most feminine woman I know." His voice caressed her, while his eyes undressed her by candlelight.

"Am I, now?" She pushed back playfully. "And how can I be of service to a man who has everything?"

"I don't quite know where to start." Douglas carved his tenderloin thoughtfully. "But you see," he said, "it's my wife."

"Your wife?" Melissa giggled, attempting to lighten the mood and maintain the pretense that she already knew he was married. "Are you stumped for what to buy her for her birthday?"

"No…no." Douglas stammered like a man who wasn't accustomed to being at a loss for words. "I just can't get through to her anymore."

"Go on." Melissa fixed her face as though she were seriously considering some expert advice to offer.

"I don't know how to say this." Douglas hesitated. "But she's a…slob—"

"No—" Melissa's breath caught in her throat. "With all of your resources at her disposal?"

"Well, to be more to the point," Douglas said grudgingly, "she's not willing to adjust to our new lifestyle…and help me grow my business."

"Oh, I see." Melissa's lavish eyes widened.

"We met when we were young. I was in grad school at Vanderbilt. She was waiting tables down in the West End." Douglas explained. "But even with our differences, we hit it off. We talked of my business aspirations, and she was all for it. When we got married, she quit her job and helped me get Star Music Promotions off the ground. She was very supportive…at first…but then the kids came…we moved to this exclusive side of town…and she just doesn't seem to fit in anymore—"

"Kids?" Melissa stared at his wedding band in a brand new light. "I didn't know you had kids—"

"How could you know?" Douglas sat down his knife and fork. "Wanza refuses to bring them to church, or let them come with me." He exhaled loudly. "She simply refuses!"

"Wanza?" Melissa's fine brows spiked at what she considered to be a name of ghetto-fabulous origin. And who better than she to know since it was a well-kept family secret that her own mother had grown up in the Knoxville projects. "Your wife's name is Wanza?"

"Yes." Douglas looked less than happy. "Wanza Johnson-Grand."

"So why won't she let your children—" Melissa eyed him for clarification.

"I have two sons." Douglas brightened. "Derek 10 and Donovan 6."

"Okay." Melissa repeated. "Why won't your wife, Wanza—" She couldn't help rolling her eyes. "Why won't she permit Derek and Donovan to attend church with you?"

"Because she's dead-set against it, and when Wanza gets like that she won't budge—about anything!" Douglas snapped. "She says the boys should accept Jesus on their own terms, if at all, when they're much older. She says, 'I don't want you or nobody else cramming that religious mess down their throats.'" Douglas mimicked his wife's sassy delivery until he noticed some disapproving glances from some of the other wealthy patrons.

"Oh, I see." Melissa nodded.

"And that's another thing." Douglas was on a roll, now. "I've tried to talk Wanza into going back to college to complete her degree, or something, so she can improve…her verbal skills…her style…her finesse." He slowed. "But she refuses. She says, 'I talked like this when you bed and wed me. If it was good enough for you then, it better be good enough for you now.'"

"But you have sophisticated clients now—"

"Exactly!" Douglas lifted his chin toward heaven with an injured stare. "You get it, Melissa. Why can't she?"

"But you said she's a slob?"

"She is!" Douglas fumed. "I'm ashamed to bring clients into my own home because I don't know what kind of wreck it'll be when we get there."

"But you do have two, young boys." Melissa attempted to appear fair. "And I'm sure they can be quite a handful—"

"I also have a housekeeper, a pool guy, and any other help she needs in that 5,000 square foot Colonial monstrosity we live in. But she still finds a way to keep our home looking like a train wreck!" Douglas pouted. "I think she does it on purpose, just to aggravate me."

"But why would she do that?" Melissa empathized. "She knows you're building…an empire."

"She hates the idea of my success." Douglas' nostrils flared. "She was okay with it when we were small. But now that we're breaking into the bigs, she says it's breaking up our family. It's pulling us apart." He pushed away his rich dessert, untouched. "But I say it's her that's killing off our family."

"Wow!" Melissa said coyly. "It does sound like you have one, big problem."

"I know." Douglas sounded more self-conscious, now. "And I don't know what to do about it."

"Have you tried counseling—"

"Wanza won't go—"

"Tutors—"

"You're kidding, right?"

"What about her friends?" Melissa's eyes flashed as if she'd stumbled upon a winner. "Maybe one of them could talk some sense into her."

"Friends?" Douglas huffed. "Wanza doesn't have friends. Nobody wants to come within a mile of *the-loud-mouth-of-the-south*, and no one wants to be seen in public with her. She dresses like she shops at the Goodwill!"

"Then, I don't know what to say." Melissa's words crossed her lips as smooth as hot butter. "Sounds like you've got a real problem on your hands."

"Well, I guess I didn't bring you here tonight to solve my problems." Douglas' sexy voice dropped into a low gear, and he added an easy smile. "I just wanted a cultured lady, such as yourself, to help me consider it."

Melissa lowered her eyes in the candlelight rather than return his intense gaze. "Oh, I see," she whispered.

Douglas reached across the table and touched her hand. The crackle of electricity that passed between them put the candlelight to shame. "I was hoping," he whispered huskily, "you'd join me in my suite…at the Hotel Carlisle…it's nearby…and we can talk over my situation in more detail—"

"And look over the church's first quarter numbers?" Melissa's heart raced like she was on an interview for the biggest job of her life.

"And look over the church's first quarter numbers," Douglas repeated, one sexy syllable at a time.

Melissa eased her hands back into her lap. "Then I don't see why not." Her eyes flamed like the flickering candlelight, and her breath thickened with lustful expectation.

"Check!" Douglas blared at the snooty waiter.

CHAPTER 1

Fool's Gold

"Here she comes, again!" Melissa Grand spun her elegant neck around and nudged her husband who was sitting on the end of the pew on the third row at True Vine Ministries, Inc. The couple was still sporting their newly-wed status, having been married for less than a year. Melissa was dripping in diamonds and pearls, looking very much the wife of one of the most influential promoters in the music industry.

"And what do you want me to do about it?" Douglas Grand groaned without bothering to turn his handsome head.

"Well, she's dragging your boys behind her." Melissa hissed.

Douglas' neck snapped around, and he smiled at his two sons who were sitting with his ex-wife three rows behind them on the opposite side of the aisle.

Derek and Donovan smiled and waved back at their daddy. Wanza Johnson-Grand, on the other hand, pushed back the blonde bangs on her brunette wig and shot Douglas a disinterested stare. She was sure he'd get her message: "Yeah, we're here, Chump! And whatcha gonna do about it?"

Douglas eased back around to face the pulpit. "Yes, I see what you mean," he said to Melissa in a raspy whisper. "She's here alright and just as ornery as ever."

"Do you see what she has on?" Melissa buzzed. "A floral sundress…with the back out, no less, and it's not even summer, yet. OMG! And at her size…so highly inappropriate for church!"

"What else is new?" Douglas deadpanned.

"Why's she doing this?" Melissa whined. "She never came to church when she was married to you. She wouldn't even let you bring the boys to church. So why's she doing it, now?"

"Guess she's trying to make a point with you, Mrs. Grand." Douglas teased, examining the deep lines etching their way into his wife's pretty face. "She's trying to get under your skin, and it looks like it's working."

"Well, this is *our* church." Melissa wrestled to compose herself. "If she must go to church, she should find somewhere else." She huffed. "And you should tell her so, Douglas. Put her in her place, once and for all."

"Fat chance!" Douglas snarled and set his eyes on the podium. Through a haze of growing anger, he saw Pastor Clarence Meadows mount the pulpit and start babbling something about starting a new series on *The Good Samaritan.* "The un-saved man in the Bible who had more love and compassion in his little finger than all the church-folk of that day had in their whole hand."

Douglas snuck a peek back at Wanza. The boys were fast asleep, and she had her eyes glued on the pastor, who was booming out something over the hushed congregation like, "And Jesus Christ is our example of love today. Amen!" *Whatever.*

When the worship service was completed, Douglas and the deacons stood in line to congratulate Pastor Meadows on a fine sermon. Douglas knew as Chairman of the Finance Committee this was expected of him, even though he hadn't made sense of a word the preacher had said.

Since Melissa had relinquished her position on the Finance Committee when she married Douglas, she kept her place in the pew. She was seething as she watched Wanza Johnson-Grand and her two sons march out of the front door like they owned the place, taking their own sweet time to place their tithing envelopes into the box. *The way she's dressed she should slither out of one of the back exits.* Melissa's brain seized with agitation. *And look at those poor boys. With all that money Douglas pays her, you'd think she'd dress them better. Their little suits look so outdated. Trifling woman! Ugh!*

When Douglas returned to the pew to join his bride, she jumped at his touch. "Not expecting me?" He teased.

"No. It's not that." Melissa intoned, employing a revised tactic. "I was thinking how important it is for you to get this thing straight with Wanza before her presence has an opportunity to embarrass you in front of the whole church…and your upscale clients who worship here." She fluttered her lavish lashes convincingly. "If you'll remember, Rapper E-Z and Bluesman Slim only joined because you're a member."

"You think that's possible?" Douglas reevaluated his wife's concern, since building his client base and expanding his music empire were his primary objectives in life.

"Well, her coming here, dressed like that…and not having your sons properly attired…could create image problems for you down the road." Melissa blew out a heavy sigh. "After all, she represents you. She is your ex-wife."

"I see what you mean." Douglas agreed. "Come on," he said. "Maybe we can catch up with her before they get away. She usually hangs around making a nuisance of herself out front."

Melissa hung back on the broad front steps of the magnificent, white church edifice, while Douglas grabbed his ex-wife's elbow and nudged her to one side of the brick-paved walkway. "Wanza!" He blared in a hoarse whisper. "What are you doing here? Why do you keep coming here?"

"It's a church, ain't it?" Wanza snatched back her elbow. "Anybody can come."

"But why here? Why now?" Douglas implored, as his sons looked on wide-eyed.

"If you had stayed away and left me alone, I would o' left you alone—you and your bougie, new wife." Wanza cranked her neck. "But nooo." She droned. "As good as you felt, you moved back into the Brentwood Estates. You buy a big ole Colonial mansion right

13

down the street from the one you bought for me, and you put your new, man-stealing wife in it. But I'm sorry to tell ya, Mister, Legend's Way ain't big enough for the both of us!"

"But, Wanza, be reasonable," Douglas said, startled at her keen perception. He'd done exactly what she'd accused him of just to show her he could do whatever he pleased, and there was nothing she could do about it. He was guilty as charged, but he never expected her to catch on quite so fast. But he should've figured she'd find a way to turn the tables on him. She always did. "But I only moved back on Legend's Way so I could be closer to the boys." Douglas alibied. "If they should need me for anything, I'll be right here—"

"Need you!" Wanza fumed. "Why should they need you? You ain't never worried 'bout them before. You hardly came home when you lived there. And it was you that left the boys behind; remember?" She caught her breath. "And since the judge forced you to pay me alimony *and* child support—after you took me to court trying to get out of it—I don't have to work no more. I'm here with the boys all the time to make sure they don't need nothing!" She flexed her neck. "Like always, I take care of my boys. So get over yourself, D-o-u-g." She drew out the shortcut of his name, long and hard, because she knew he hated it. "I don't need you, and these boys don't need you—anymore. You just pick 'em up on your assigned weekends, and we'll be cool."

"And you won't come back to True Vine anymore?" Douglas pressed his point.

"Can't promise you that." Wanza flashed a wicked smile in Melissa's direction. "Your new wife may need to keep in mind who came first...and who's the boss." She drilled. "You should o' stayed on over there in them swanky condos with your li'l bougie woman after you left me. You had no business coming back on Legend's Way!"

"But Wanza." Douglas groaned, realizing he was getting nowhere fast. "My church is here; my kids are here; my business is nearby. This is my neighborhood, too."

"I know you don't think much o' me." Wanza's voice sizzled. "Naw, I don't have no superfied job, or no Ivy League education, but I worked hard enough with two kids on my hip to help you finish your MBA and start yo' business, Mr. Doug. And I'll have you know, I can be anywhere, any time, and you ain't got nothing to say about it." Wanza pulled her boys close to her thick hips. "And if you don't want me to lose my mind right here on the front steps of your precious True Vine Church, you'd better back up off me, Mister, and get up out my face!" Wanza turned on a dime, and the boys nearly stumbled over her chunky ankles. "Have a blessed day, D-o-u-g." She sneered in Melissa's direction. "You and yours!"

CHAPTER 2
Golden Glitter

Melissa awoke Monday morning with a deep, cat-like stretch to find Douglas packing his twin Gucci bags. She and her husband had had a long eventful night of lovemaking, and her mind was still dancing with sugarplums from the things he said. *And the things he did. Oh, my!* Since their very first night together at the Hotel Carlisle, they had always done their best communicating between the sheets. And she was in no hurry to move out of her warm spot in their luxurious, king-sized bed. The IRS wouldn't see her today; she'd call in sick. It was one of the many perks of her new station in life, and she planned to use every one of them to the fullest. "Morning, Babe." Melissa yawned cozily. "Where're you off to today?"

"Morning, Beautiful." Douglas winked. "Got to make a trip out to the Left Coast for a few days."

"L.A., again?"

"Nope. San Francisco this time and maybe a stop in San Diego. Got to sign up this new rapper kid, Tomm Katt, who's ready to take it to the next level, and he needs me and Star Music Promotions *International* to make it happen."

"And how's that working out for you?" Melissa teased.

"You mean the *International* part?" Douglas smirked. "Well, I've got to speak it into being; right? Besides, I've got New York and L.A. pretty much sewed up, now. You don't have to sign-up Beyoncé to make it big in this business. You've just got to corner the market on all the rest of the young talent out there. And that's me, Babe. That's me." His chest swelled. "I'm promoting the cream of the crop—Blues, R&B, Rap, Rock, Pop, Hip-Hop—you name it. And I want Star to be a full-service agency, a one-stop shop. I want these young artists to be able to get anything and everything they need…from me. I want to own them—"

"Oh, I see." Melissa blinked.

"And I've got my first trip planned to London next month." Douglas boasted. "I think some of our up-and-coming artists can make good music over there. So I'm getting there—"

"We're…getting there." Melissa fluttered her pretty eyes.

"Well, yeah," Douglas said, with a trickle of sarcasm floating just under the surface. "Always."

"Have you ever thought we should move back to Oakland where you're from?"

"Nope," Douglas said without hesitation. "I'm perfectly comfortable with Nashville as my home base. Don't forget; I cut my baby teeth signing up the blues singers in this town, and they don't let me forget it, either. Besides, where we are physically doesn't matter anymore. You know that. We're all connected in the Cloud. I've got a great staff in place. I can do my business from anywhere, and I like Music City USA."

"But if we were to relocate to New York or L.A., you'd be closer to some of your clients—"

"And I'd be further away from others—"

"But we'd be further away from Wanza and all her mess—"

"And I'd be further away from my kids," Douglas said sternly. "I don't want that."

"But Douglas—"

"I pay Wanza her money." Douglas bristled. "We're cool."

"But Babe, if she keeps showing up at our church, her very presence could tarnish your reputation with some of your major clients, Pastor Meadows, the Finance Committee—"

"No worries, Douglas said proudly. "My position at True Vine is a lock. With my lucrative tithes and my business expertise, I'm a natural as Chairman of the Finance Committee. Nobody can challenge that—"

"But Douglas—"

"Enough!" Douglas whipped the zipper closed on his luggage. "I'm building my empire from Nashville. It's never been done before, and I'm going to do it. I'm going to stay close to my kids. And I *will* take my business international!"

CHAPTER 3

Golden Streams

Melissa had a big pot of decaf coffee brewing in her expansive kitchen when she heard the quiet tap-tap on her front door. Her brother was a recovering addict, and she didn't want to put any more drugs into his system, not even caffeine. Plus, she figured the coffee would help because he was always fighting an uphill battle with demon rum, which he just couldn't seem to kick. When Melissa opened the door, his stingy-brimmed hat glided onto the floor like a wobbly frisbee. "Coast clear, Missy?" he whispered.

"Get in here, Boy!" Melissa giggled. Her brother could always make her laugh.

"Just checkin'." He rounded the corner with his trademark toothpick wedged into a jagged smile, baggy jeans and short, dark locks. At 38, he was two years older, but about the same height as Melissa. Even as a child, he was like this old soul trapped in a young man's body. Somehow, he felt things—sensed things—more deeply than most of his peers. His rugged good looks and mannish charm had a way of getting him into as many scrapes as it pulled him out of, and that hadn't changed. But his years behind bars had hardened his personality, and the off-and-on years of alcohol and drug abuse had contributed to his scrawny frame. The slight limp in his right knee from his glory days as a high school running back seemed to be worsening with time, but he did his best to camouflage it with a cool lean and a dap step. It was his way, making light of circumstances that would've carried a weaker man under. "You know," he said in his slick, easy style, "I swore I'd never step foot in this joint, again; not after my one-and-only meet-and-greet with that husband o' yours."

"I told you; Douglas is away on business today." Melissa swooped up his hat and pressed it back into his needle-scarred hands with a comforting squeeze. "And I'm glad to have my big brother all to myself. I've got some coffee for us in the kitchen."

"Besides, with all them big, ole columns 'cross your front porch out there, Miss Missy," he said, needling her, "I feel like I need to come in shufflin' and sangin' Dixie."

"You're a nut!" Melissa grinned. "Sit down. I'll pour you a cup."

"But I ain't playing, Missy." He chomped down on his toothpick. "I don't get no good vibes off that husband o' yours. 'Cause try as he might, he can't hide all that arrogance under a three-piece suit."

"Ha-Ha." Melissa smirked. "Well, if you hadn't been in *jail* last year when I got married, Dear Brother, maybe you could've put in your two-cents worth—not that it would've done you any good. Douglas is the man of my dreams." She tossed back her dark, flowing curls. "And I've earned the right to have what I want—"

"Uh-huh. I can see it all, now." Her brother flicked his toothpick from side to side. "The preacher saying, 'Speak now or forever hold yo' peace.' And me hollering out, 'Hey, Judge-Yo-Honor, I object!'"

"Well, your objections have been overruled." Melissa sat the hot brew at his place in her stylish breakfast nook. "Douglas is my husband. I love him. And it's going to stay that way—forever."

"Yo' funeral," he quipped. "So…why did you call me over to this God-forsaken place, anyhow?"

"Because it's better than that rat-hole you live in." Melissa gave him as good as she got.

"Well, I'm just getting back on my feet." Her brother smiled sheepishly. "And I owe it all to prison overcrowding, good behavior and, of course, to you—for sponsoring my five-year parole and getting me that thankless job downtown as a janitor." He flipped back his stingy-brimmed hat, and one of his locks popped up, like he was trying out as a vaudeville comedian. "And all this behind your beloved husband's back, I might add." He tacked on a silly wink. "But you've always been a sneaky little cuss; now, ain't you, Missy?"

"Shh!" Melissa set her finger across her sassy lips. "That's our own little secret; remember?"

"Any-hoo." Her brother deadpanned. "Whatzup? You sounded a hot mess over the phone."

"Wanza Johnson-Grand." Melissa plunked down a big slice of cake next to his mug. "That's what's up!"

"Who dat?" He set his toothpick aside and stirred in mega amounts of sugar into his coffee, no cream. He took a big bite of cake.

"Douglas' ex-wife!" Melissa hissed. "She keeps showing up at our church—"

"That a fact?"

"Just last Sunday, she came swirling into the sanctuary looking like a shrink-wrapped super blimp in that spandex halter dress—pulling those two munchkins behind her. They look like the three bears, or something. All of them are so grossly overweight. Ugh! There ought to be a law against over-feeding your kids." Melissa steamed. "Anyway, there they sit, three rows behind us on the other side of the aisle—glaring. It makes me so uncomfortable, but Douglas refuses to do anything about it."

"What you want the man to do, Missy?"

"Handle his business!" She snapped. "Keep that riff-raft out of our midst—especially on Sunday mornings."

"Have you ever tried to talk to her?" He chewed thoughtfully. "Reason with her?"

"You can't talk to that woman." Melissa fumed. "All she does is rant about how Douglas mistreated her and her boys. You can't get through to her."

"Then I suggest you just back off." He flexed his back against the chair. "If she sees her presence doesn't faze you, she'll get bored with showing up at church on Sunday mornings." He stretched out his sore knee. "Who in their right mind wants to get up early on Sunday mornings, anyhow? Daddy didn't wanna do it, and he was the preacher—"

"But Mama sure made him." Melissa clucked. "I can hear her screaming, now, as she left out of her bedroom and went into his. 'Get up out of that bed right this minute, Walter Mann.' She mimicked her mother's prissy tone, which was sharpened with a demanding edge. 'Do you forget you're the Shepherd of the Flock; the Senior Pastor at Faith Freewill of Knoxville? You have to set the example, set the pace. You weren't complaining when you stayed up all night playing that stupid—Solitaire. So get up out of that bed this instant!'"

"Yeah, and I could hear Daddy from my room next door, too." Her brother grinned. "And he'd be cussing her out under his breath as soon as she turned her back."

"Not our Daddy?" Melissa flapped her hand across her heart in feigned amazement.

"Yes, our Daddy." Her brother shot her the eye. "And you know it, too, Missy. Don't play with me."

"As I recall," Melissa said, "Mother kept all of us in church—all day Sunday and Wednesday nights, too. That's why I promised myself when I moved to Nashville, I'd never set foot into another church—"

"Back at ya!"

"But then I found True Vine…over here in the high-rent district." Melissa giggled. "I liked Pastor Meadows. And then I met Douglas, and the rest is history."

"I don't know what you see in that weenie—"

"I love Douglas." Melissa defended. "But there's no one else I can talk to about that woman but you, Money—"

"Ah-h, just hearing you say my name is music to my ears," her brother said. "And for that alone, I guess I still owe you—"

"For what?"

"I haven't forgotten how they tortured me all through grade school because of my name—"

"LaMonte—"

"Do-not-use-that-name-in-my-presence-again!" Money gritted his teeth like she was scraping a thumbnail against a chalkboard. "Because of that name, kids called me Preacher Fag; Sissy Mann...and worse. For a while there, I didn't think I was gonna make it to middle school. I was desperate enough to—"

"Well, it was Daddy who let Mother name you after her father and me after her mother—"

"Yeah, it was just like Daddy to knuckle down under that woman," Money exclaimed. "He had to know a name like that was gonna get me killed at Harriet Tubman Elementary, and he did absolutely nothing about it for six long years—"

"I'm just glad you couldn't say Melissa when I was born." His sister winked. "Because you're the only person on the planet I allow to call me Missy."

"And I'm glad you fixed my problem before I lost my mind—"

"Well, I overheard Deacon Goody trying to convince Daddy that what he was doing wasn't gambling. 'Because all my horses come in on the money,' he'd said. And that's when I realized it—everybody loves money. And if your name was Money, they'd love you, too."

You were only in the 4th grade. I was in the 6th. But when you started calling me Money Mann in the halls that day, the kids stopped calling me Sissy Mann, just like that." He snapped his fingers. "And since they thought it was my idea, I became the smart one. And from that day, we became *The Mighty Manns*—Money and

Melissa—brains & beauty." Money bragged. "Even the teachers started treating me differently. Brilliant idea, Missy. Just brilliant! You saved my life—"

"And, now, Money Mann," Melissa said, gently tracing the crude prison tattoos etched across his tortured hands, "I need your help, too."

"You got it, Missy. Me and you—the two of us—like always!" Money declared. "Nobody messes with these Preacher's Kids and gets away with it. Nobody!" Money tweaked her nose like when they were kids. "If you wanna hang onto that tired-piece man o' yours," Money said, gagging, "then I'm all in." He re-seated his toothpick, rubbed his bad knee and stood. Slowly, he swiveled 360 degrees to take in the cold grandeur of the elegantly-appointed open floor plan, which was, undeniably, branded by the *Mann-touch*—white baby grand piano; crystal chandeliers; priceless antiques; heavy red drapes; and an imposing, floor-to-ceiling, specially-commissioned oil painting of the happy couple in a gilded frame. "But promise me one thang, Missy." Money strolled out with his cool pimp-limp. "Don't make me have to step foot back into this painted pony...not ever, again."

"Promise," Melissa whispered.

CHAPTER 4

Gold Rush

The next Sunday, Pastor Meadows was midway in his series on *The Good Samaritan*. He'd been booming over the congregation all morning about the virtues of loving their neighbor and extending a hand to strangers who couldn't repay their acts of kindness. "For if you're saved and sanctified today," he said, "it's because the Lord looked upon you with eyes of mercy and chose to extend His hand of love to you." He appealed passionately. "It's not because you're good. It's because Jesus has the power to forgive you of your sins and keep you until the day you see Him face-to-face. We can never repay His grace and mercy, but we can certainly share His love with others we meet."

Pastor Meadows commanded their attention, alright, because his round, bald head resembled a tan soccer ball with black, bushy eyebrows precariously attached, and nobody wanted to miss it if they ever fell off. That prospect alone was mesmerizing, especially for those catching the close-ups on the jumbotron. But unlike many of his fellow mega-preachers, he'd never quite mastered the art of hooping and whipping the congregation up into a frenzied fury. Instead, Pastor Meadows relied on what he'd been given to get the message across—his big heart, his big voice, and his uncompromising faith in sound doctrine.

No sooner than the pastor had extended the altar call, a young woman came running and wailing from the rear of the church. She was tugging on the hand of the little boy who was trailing behind her. All eyes followed them as they made their way to Pastor Meadows who was standing bug-eyed in front of the pulpit. And this was not a good look for him; since with his rock-hard physique and squat statue, he more resembled a heavyweight prize fighter who'd been sucker-punched, than the compassionate pastor of one of the largest growing congregations in the country.

The young woman fell at his feet crying, "Are you the Good Samaritan, Pastor? 'Cause I sure do need him, now!"

The congregation sucked in its collective breath. Many of the affluent heads across the 3,000-plus audience began to droop like day lilies on a hot afternoon; at least, those that weren't hightailing it for the exists in mortal fear of their safety.

"What is she doing?" Melissa buzzed in Douglas' ear. "There's no place in the order of service for this! This is an altar call, not a reality show. OMG!"

"Shh!" Douglas brushed his wife away with a flick of his head. He didn't want to miss a moment of this highly-charged, unexpected drama.

Pastor Meadows reached down, self-consciously, and helped the young woman onto her feet. She was dressed shabbily in boy-cut jeans and a camouflage hunting jacket with the sleeves cut out. The tee she had on underneath revealed that she was braless; and her distended belly button, which protruded through the thin cotton fabric, revealed that she was pregnant. She was built straight up and down, so she resembled a sausage link with a big knot tied in the middle. The little boy with her was clean, but his little pants were flooding above his ankles, and his shirt was at least two sizes too large. She had on dollar-store flip flops. The little boy's feet were bare.

"What is it, my child," Pastor Meadows said to her in his most fatherly tone, which was barely audible except for those nearest the front row.

Douglas and Melissa could hear, and their eyes and ears were glued on the exchange.

A few rows back, Wanza was straining to hear. *Man, this is better than Geraldo*!

"I need help," the young woman said to Pastor Meadows. She was rubbing her short hair, which was slicked tight to her head, and her eyes were brimming over with tears. "I was headed outta town. My car gave outta gas…right here in front o' yo' church. I have no money. I had no choice but to bring the baby in out the heat. We sat in the back." She picked up the little boy into her arms. "Your sign says you're serving lunch today. He hungry. We hungry." She wailed. "We need yo' help!"

"Now-now, Daughter," Pastor Meadows said consolingly. "You're safe here. What's your name?"

"Yteesha." She drew in her breath. "Yteesha Sereeta Lee. And this here's my son, Austin Yontee Lee. I'm twenty. He two."

"Well, it's a pleasure to meet you Yteesha and Austin." Pastor Meadows offered his thick index finger to the little boy who promptly held on tight. "And we're going to see what we can do to help you. Is that alright?"

"Yes, sir," Yteesha said respectfully. "That's quite alright."

"At such short notice, Yteesha, I don't think I can go through our normal channels to get you placed today." Pastor Meadows thought for a moment. "But if I can get someone in here to help you, like The Good Samaritan, would you be willing to accept their kindness."

"Sure." Yteesha whimpered. She was so tired and humiliated she could barely stand. She placed Austin onto the floor, and he grabbed onto Pastor Meadow's robe with his tiny fist.

"Brothers and Sisters." Pastor Meadows turned to his startled congregation. "We have a unique, but not uncommon, situation here today."

The congregation nodded in varying degrees of agreement; their curiosity almost palpable.

"This is Yteesha Lee and her young son, Austin." Pastor Meadows continued. The little boy cooed at the mention of his name, and the sound of his voice eased the tension in the startled sanctuary. "Yteesha and Austin have fallen on hard times," the pastor said. "The same thing that could happen to any one of us has happened to them—the same thing that happened to the man who was beset by robbers and who was helped by The Good Samaritan."

The thinning congregation nodded in recognition of the similarities.

"And we're being called on this morning to be that Good Samaritan," Pastor Meadows proclaimed. "Maybe, it's God's way of testing each of us to see if we understand the significance of putting His love into action in His church."

A sigh of recognition flooded through the congregation as they saw where the Pastor was heading, and the sea of eyes was bobbling in all directions. The pastor pressed on. "Yteesha and Austin need someone, some family to take them into their home for several days until we can find suitable placement for them in one of our partnering agencies." Pastor Meadows cleared his throat when he saw his appeal was falling on deaf ears. "Like I say," the pastor clarified, "this act of kindness will only take up a few days of your time and then—"

"I'll do it!" Wanza hopped up from her seat. She cast her gaze over the sanctuary to see firsthand what she'd suspected. Most of the congregation had their heads buried in their Bibles, or they were tipping for the exits. "I'll do it," Wanza repeated. "They can come home with me, Preacher." She scraped her eyes over Douglas and Melissa. "I've got plenty good room at my house—it's just me and my boys—and Yteesha and Austin can stay as long as they like."

"Come up here." Pastor Meadows beckoned for Wanza to join them. She left Derek and Donovan asleep on the pew and sauntered up to the front of the room. She was wearing a red sheath dress, which showed off lots of cleavage on the top and rolling waves of cellulite on the bottom. And she was sporting a long, two-toned wig that coordinated with her outfit.

Melissa jabbed Douglas in the ribs with her elbow. "What's Wanza trying to prove?" She fumed. "She's not even a member here!"

"Not now!" Douglas warned in a raspy whisper; eyes still glued on the strange proceedings.

"Hey, Girl," Wanza said when she reached the front, hugging Yteesha's skinny frame like they were old friends. "No worries." Wanza added. "I've got boys of my own. It's gonna be alright." The church clerk sprang up from her hiding place to log-in their personal information.

"Well, I don't know if anybody else feels like praising the Lord afresh." Pastor Meadows heralded. "But I do!" And with that, he began clapping his thick, strong hands and glorifying God until the remaining congregation was standing on its feet to join him.

No sooner than the clapping had died down and everyone was taking their seats, another woman was making her way down the center aisle toward Pastor Meadows. Wanza and Yteesha parted like the Red Sea and stood on one side of Pastor Meadows to watch this young, white woman make her way to the front.

True Vine was an interracial congregation so the occurrence was not at all rare. But Pastor Meadows was as taken aback as the rest of the men in the audience as this young woman made her way forward. She was a ravishing beauty of about 30—with a buxom bosom, like Dolly; porcelain white features, like the Greek goddess, Athena; and a flaming halo of long, wavy red hair, like Xena the Gaelic warrior princess. She was wearing jeweled boots and a fringed jacket and skirt. Pastor Meadows had to close his mouth before he could open it, again, and say, "Welcome," as his bushy brows swooshed upwards. "This is such an unusual day," he said, "I must ask why you've come forward at this time?"

"Who is she?" Melissa buzzed in Douglas' ear.

Douglas pushed away from Melissa. He sat up tall in the pew and hung onto this beautiful woman's every word.

"Good morning, Pastor. I'm Willamina," the young lady said gently, "Willamina Redd."

With that, a few gasps of recognition poured over the congregation. They knew her as the Grammy-nominated, rising star of County music fame—the nouveaux Belle of Nashville. Of course, Douglas recognized the name, but he'd never expected she'd be such a total babe.

"And I've come forward this morning," Miss Redd went on to say, "to join this fine congregation." She smiled and the whole room lit up. "I'm from Texas, you know, but I make my home in this neighborhood when I'm in town. And I've been coming here, off and on, for some time. But after seeing the authenticity of this ministry and the awesome move of God in this place this morning, I'm compelled to join up with y'all."

"Well, my sister, we are so glad to have you." Pastor Meadows gleefully cranked her hand. "And from your profession of faith, I presume you're coming by Christian Experience."

"I am," she said quietly.

"Then, Sister Willamina Redd," Pastor Meadows bellowed, "it will be our delight to offer you the right hand of fellowship this morning."

"Thank you, Pastor."

Willamina Redd turned to face the congregation, and Douglas Grand's eyeballs bulged out of their sockets. Every part of his body was responding to this gorgeous woman with lustful desire. And from this first sighting, his ears were pinned back to get next to Miss Redd. Melissa, on the other hand, was far too busy fuming over the unorthodoxy of the day's proceedings to notice that her husband had been totally captivated by the newest member of True Vine Ministries, Inc.

After the benediction, Douglas went back to the Finance room for a called meeting. Pastor Meadows and the leadership team greeted Miss Redd up front. And Wanza and Yteesha passed by Melissa's pew on their way back to pick up her boys.

"And, now, there're two of them," Melissa muttered under her breath.

"Two what?" Wanza jumped her.

"Huh?" Melissa was startled. She knew she'd thought it, but she didn't realize she'd said it.

But Wanza didn't let it go. "You mean, two women that's got more class in their two fingers than you've got in your whole body?"

"But I—"

"Two women who'd jump yo' skinny behind if we weren't in the church-house?" Wanza persisted.

"Wait a minute." Melissa bounced back in her own defense. "I'm not the one—"

"Naw!" Wanza snatched the words out of her mouth and twirled them into the air. "You're the one that stole my husband and made orphans outta my two, little boys. That's who you are!"

"I didn't steal your husband!" Melissa's voice scratched like a cat's paw. "Douglas was looking to unload you when I met him. I didn't even know you existed—"

"You didn't know I existed?" Wanza's multi-colored wig stood on end. "So what did you think that wide, gold wedding band on his left hand stood for, huh?" She set her hands on her wide hips. "But, my bad, I forgot…a wedding band is a turn-on for a cheap trick like you!"

"Now, you hold on just one minute!" Melissa's voice shrilled and her slender neck flipped out of its socket. "Douglas didn't even wear that *wide, gold wedding band* when I met him." She peppered. "Guess he didn't want people knowing he had a worthless cow like *you* tucked away—"

"Grrrr!" Wanza lunged at Melissa. "I'm gon' slap the taste out yo' mouth!" But in the nick of time, Yteesha managed to grab a handful of her skintight dress to restrain her. When Wanza whirled around, her dangling earring popped her in one eye and in the other was the reflection of three sets of frightened little eyes, and Yteesha Lee's big mouth hanging wide open.

"Come on, Miss Wanza." Yteesha gathered up all the kids and pushed her toward the door. "Let's go."

Willamina Redd came up from the rear and put an arm around Wanza and Yteesha. "Yes, ladies," she whispered, "this is neither the time nor the place."

"Don't worry." Wanza pulled her wig back into place. "We're going. But this ain't over…not by a long shot."

Melissa smoothed her sleek, black hair and bobbled her neck back into its proper orbit, while Miss Redd eased the women and the boys toward the front door. Meanwhile, some of the remaining members of the congregation stood by dumbfounded, having witnessed such an incredible spectacle in the hallowed sanctuary of True Vine Ministries, Inc.

CHAPTER 5
Gold Record

Melissa had already grabbed a table for them at the Howlin' Moon Blues Café when her brother cruised through the door, looking as cool and dapper as ever. The lunchtime crowd in the popular hangout was starting to pick up. An old-fashioned jukebox in the corner was bellowing out country music, and Melissa had to wave at Money to get his attention. "Over here," she called.

"Oh, hey, Missy." Money slid into the booth across from her. "You rang?"

"Yes, I did." Melissa flapped. "I needed to see you."

"About your li'l problem, huh?" Money put his head on a swivel to be sure no one else was listening.

"Yes." Melissa carped. "She did it, again!"

"What this time?" Money chewed on his toothpick.

"Wanza actually threatened me…in the middle of the church's sanctuary…in front of witnesses!" Melissa gave Money the blow-by-blow of the previous Sunday's shenanigans. "Can you believe that?"

"Sure, I can believe it." Money casually eyed the menu.

"But with a name like Wanza and her public housing background, I guess I should've expected it wouldn't be long before she'd resort to violence—"

"Now, don't go there, Missy…not with the name calling, and all. I mean…really?" He gave her a long, hard look. "You know our own mother grew up in the Knoxville projects—"

"And now I see why she hounded Daddy night and day to be a super pastor, so she'd never have to go back."

"Yeah, well, that might've been one of the reasons she made the man's life a living hell." Money paused as the waiter came and went. "But your situation reminds me of the time I had to keep Lola

Lumpkin from kickin' your behind." Money slurped his decaf coffee with a wicked twinkle in his eye.

"Lola Lumpkin?" Melissa's elegant eyes flashed. "Why would you bring that up at a time like this?"

"If you'll recall, you stole her boyfriend, too." Money crowed. "You were a lowly sophomore. She was a senior. And if I hadn't stepped in when I did, she would o' stomped you into a mud puddle."

"See, that's my point." Melissa seethed. "I didn't steal Lola's boyfriend from her, any more than I stole Douglas from Wanza. The boy came after me."

"Yeah, but you knew he'd been Lola's man all through high school—"

"But is it my fault that I was smarter and prettier than Lola Lumpkin?" Melissa pushed back her long, dark curls from her splendid face.

"And then you had to go and slash all her tires when no one was looking—"

"Well, it served her right, and it's not my fault, Money." Melissa's voice scratched. "You know how nutty-brained I get when somebody tries to mess over me."

"And when the po' boy came crawling back to you, you only took him back so you could dog him out that much more—"

"Well, it served him right, too, for acting like such a wimp—"

"For acting like Daddy, you mean," Money blurted.

"Let's not go there." Melissa's eyes warned. "Let's leave the past in the past; shall we?"

"Okay." Money shrugged. "But I'm just sayin' that's the way you roll. And if I hadn't taken the rap for the tires you slashed, they would've stripped your crown, *Miss Homecoming Queen*."

"I know that." Melissa pursed her perky lips. "And I'm sorry for that, Money, because it got you kicked off the ROTC squad."

"No worries." Money's jaw tightened. "I was sick o' all that hut-1, hut-2 mess, anyhow."

"You're my hero, Money." Melissa beamed. "You've always looked out for me."

"That's my job, Missy." Money winked. "Somebody's gotta."

"Well, they didn't call us PKs for nothing." Melissa chuckled, her big eyes darting mischievously.

"Yeah." Money snickered. "Partners-in-Krime."

"But unlike before, Money, I really do love Douglas—"

"Really?" Money locked her in a mind-melding stare.

"Really! And everything'll come out right this time, Money; you'll see." Melissa gave her brother a taste of her most seductive gaze. "I'll make it come out right."

"Alrighty-then." Money took a big bite of his burger, impressed by his little sister's obvious determination. "But don't the man get a say in the matter?"

"Oh, Money, stay on point." Melissa grumbled. "What am I going to do about Wanza? She could mess up everything with her trifling-self, if people find out she's Douglas' ex-wife. She doesn't look the part. She doesn't act the part. And people could think less of Douglas—and me—because of her."

Money chewed on his burger. "I had the guy I was riding with do a drive by when I came to see you the other day, seeing as how I was in the neighborhood and all."

"You drove by Wanza's?"

"I'm ya boy." Money bumped his fist across his heart. "I'll go to the trunk for ya. And just in case things between you and Wanza ever become more than war-talk, I wanted to case the joint for a return visit."

"Well, alright," Melissa said, smiling broadly at her big brother's loyalty to her and his commitment to her cause.

"But I didn't see nothing happening over there—just her, them two boys, and that big ole house." Money chewed slowly. "And, now, I guess you can add a pregnant girl and her little boy to the mix."

"Yes." Melissa agreed.

"Well then, I wouldn't worry 'bout it, Missy." Money slid back his stingy-brimmed hat and stretched out his bad knee. "Seems like Wanza ain't got much of a life."

"But she keeps showing up!" Melissa protested.

"So." Money choked down the last of his burger with a crooked smile. "Leave her alone, and she'll go home, wagging her tail behind her."

"Cute. Real cute." Melissa pursed her lips at Money's attempted humor. "So you think I've got nothing to worry about?"

"Naw, Missy." Money flipped his napkin into his empty plate. "Live your life, Girl. Be happy. I'll keep an eye on the situation."

"Okay." Melissa's forehead creased. "But there's one more matter we need to discuss."

"What's that?" Money said, signaling for a big slice of apple pie a la mode.

"We can't meet like this anymore." Melissa squirmed.

"Why not?" Money scratched at the stubble on his chin. "How will I see you?"

Melissa took a deep breath. "You see, I told Douglas you'd paid your debt to society for drug dealing, and you were on the straight-and-narrow…living in Knoxville—"

"So how did you explain my visit to your house when I met his worthless—"

"I told him you were just up for a visit to meet my new husband, and you went right back to Knoxville."

"Oh, I see." Money's eyes saddened. "Pushing ole Money to the margins, huh?"

"That's not it, Money." Melissa whined. "I love having you around, but it was the only way I could handle it so I wouldn't have to tell him I sponsored your parole right here in Nashville. Because Douglas said as soon as you left, 'I'm glad he lives in Knoxville because I can't have your drug-dealing, ex-con brother hanging around. It would be bad for business.'"

"Oh, I see."

"And I didn't tell him that this is actually your second strike—"

"Why should you?" Money fumed. "I served my time for my first strike, as you call it."

"I'll never understand why you were in on an armed robbery in the first place?" Melissa frowned.

"You mean why was a promising high school football star and honor student driving the getaway car for some stick-up artists the summer before he was going off to college?"

"Don't play with me, Money." Melissa was nearly in tears. "That senseless act cost you more than 15 years of your life. And it would've been 25, if Daddy and the church hadn't exerted their influence to get you a reduced sentence; since, at least, you had the good sense not to have a gun in your possession."

"Daddy and the rest o' them hypocrites is what drove me to it in the first place—"

"Don't give me that, Money." Melissa's brown eyes darkened.

"All of them, claiming to be so holier-than-thou at that church-house." Money's jaw clenched. "But it was a totally a different story when you followed 'em to their house—"

"That's just a cop-out, Money, and you know it." Melissa bristled.

"You tell the story your way, Missy, and I'll tell it mine." Money bobbed his head. "But I know what I'm talking 'bout."

"But more importantly," Melissa said, not giving him an inch, "we both know this *is* your second strike. And that means, Money

Mann, you cannot get a third." She breathed deeply. "In Tennessee, it's three strikes and you're out. They would put you away for life…and I couldn't stand that, Money. I just couldn't—"

"Don't worry, Missy." Money squeezed his little sister's hand. "I'm straight. I'm right as rain. There will be no third strike. I promise." He smiled boyishly. "Besides, you can't get rid of me that easy."

"Need anything?" Melissa said, as she signed the credit card slip for their lunch tab.

"Ah-h, Missy, you know me." Money shrugged.

Melissa smiled and slid a napkin in Money's direction. It had a crisp, one-hundred-dollar bill tucked away inside.

CHAPTER 6
Gold Mine

By that following Wednesday, Pastor Meadows had summoned both Wanza and Yteesha into his study at True Vine. Since his wife, Candi, served as his secretary, assistant, and at times, personal bodyguard, he felt very comfortable going solo with women there. He and Candi had met during their undergraduate days at Fisk University; married in the historic Fisk Chapel; and were joined at the hip in marriage and ministry. And since they were a childless couple, True Vine was their baby.

"How're you, Preacher." Wanza came in huffing, palming a can of soda in her right hand. "I don't know why you'd pick the hottest day in May to have this meeting?"

"I've seen better days." Pastor Meadows chuckled, attempting to disarm her bluster. "That church food we had after the Elders' meeting walked the halls of my stomach all night long." He patted his lean belly. "I've got to get back to my smoothies—"

"So you're one o' them health nuts, huh, Preacher?" Wanza took another big gulp from her can. "But these sodas are the only thing that can keep me cool."

"Well, I do what I can to stay in shape; got to keep up with this spirited congregation," he said, while keeping his seat behind the piles of paper that cluttered his desk. "But come on in and sit down." The pastor's dark, bushy eyebrows twisted as he glanced down at his scribbled notes. "Where's the other young lady? Yteesha?"

"Well, ever since she got to my house that girl ain't done nothing but eat and sleep." Wanza said, stuffing the fullness of her frame into one of his stingy guest chairs. "Guess she's tired and all. She's real pregnant, you know. Said she'd rather stay home and watch the kids."

"And what of her little boy…Austin?" Pastor Meadows smiled.

"He's fine, too." Wanza resituated her soda can and took a sip. She'd worn a long, crimson wig tipped in blonde for the occasion. "He's growing like a weed and into everything. My boys just love him. They all get along real good."

"That's good to hear." Pastor Meadows rechecked his notes. "Mrs. Johnson-Grand."

"You can just call me Wanza." She flustered. "The rest of that name is worthless, anyhow."

"Why's that?" The pastor's bushy brows knitted in a look of complete sincerity.

Wanza pushed her bangs out of her eyes and returned the favor. "So you don't know; do you, Preacher?"

"Well, I know you're not a member at True Vine." The pastor defended his depth of intimacy with his flock. "Our church clerk made me aware of that."

"No…I'm not a member here." Wanza took her time dropping the bombshell. "But—" She curled her lips. "My ex-husband is."

"Your *ex*-husband?" Pastor Meadows looked dumbfounded. He prided himself in knowing the intricate details of the lives of his congregation. Nothing got past him, and to the best of his ability, nothing got left unaddressed. "Who's your ex-husband?"

"None other than the Chairman of your Finance Committee," Wanza said, hurling his name like it was a curse word, "Douglas Grand!"

"That can't be." The pastor sparked. "I married Douglas and Melissa right here in our main sanctuary…less than a year ago. Surely he would've told me if he had a wife—"

"Don't know whether he told you are not." Wanza smarted. "Guess that's between y'all—"

"And your two sons?" Pastor Meadows checked his notes, again. "Derek and Donovan?"

"Yep." Wanza flashed the preacher a defiant look. "Douglas Grand is their daddy."

"Then I must look into this further—"

"You do that." Wanza sniffed.

"But today," Pastor Meadows said, squaring his broad shoulders, "let's talk about how we're going to help Yteesha and Austin—"

"And her unborn baby." Wanza added.

"Of course, the three of them." Pastor Meadows agreed. "Well, I've spoken to the Women's Services Center." He explained. "They're a federally-funded agency that has as its mission to help young, unwed mothers get a fresh start in life."

"Good." Wanza nodded. "That's certainly what Yteesha needs."

"Has she shared her story with you?" Pastor Meadows questioned.

"Not yet." Wanza admitted. "Like I told you, she's been doing a lot o' eating and sleeping and lying around. I've been cutting her a break 'cause I figure she's tired from what all she's been through. She'll tell me her story when she's ready—"

"Well, it's got to be soon." The pastor cautioned. "She'll have to lay out her whole situation when she goes to the Center. They'll require it."

"And when will that be?"

"It'll probably be at least two weeks before they can have a place for them—"

"Hold on, now!" Wanza raised her hand. "I'm not rushing you or nothing, Preacher. Yteesha and lil' Austin can stay with me as long as they like—"

"But we want them to be on the road to complete recovery; right?" Pastor Meadows nudged.

"Well…yes."

"So I think their situation can best be served by professionals who can give Yteesha the kind of counseling and help she needs to build a life for her and her children."

"You're right." Wanza conceded. "I'd just love on 'em and squeeze 'em to death 'cause I've got that kind o' time."

"I do want to commend you, Wanza, for opening up your heart and your home to those two." Pastor Meadows sat back and really looked her over. "You've certainly got the spirit of The Good Samaritan."

"You think so?" Wanza flushed.

"I do." The pastor reaffirmed. "But that's not all that's needed."

"Huh?" Wanza's brows creased. "Needed for what?"

"To be saved."

"What you talking 'bout, Preacher?"

"The Bible says if you confess with your mouth that Jesus is Lord, and believe in your heart that God raised Him from the dead, you shall be saved." Pastor Meadows' brows parted, and his eyes drew in on her. "Do you believe that, Wanza?"

"Well, I've listened to you every Sunday since I've been coming here, Preacher." Wanza considered thoughtfully. "And, yes, I believe Jesus loves me. And I believe He died to pay for all my sins on that cross. And I really believe He rose from the grave with all power in His hands… and…oh—" Wanza broke off suddenly.

"Yes?" Pastor Meadows coaxed quietly so as not to disturb the solemnity of the moment.

"He rose with all power in His hands…so He can help me…in the here-and-now," Wanza whispered.

"Yes." Pastor Meadows affirmed with a nod; his heart warmed by the move of the Spirit. "Then do you believe Jesus has the right to call the shots in your life?"

"Huh?"

"In other words, Wanza, do you believe that He is Lord over your life." Pastor Meadows interlaced his thick fingers, set them under his square chin and waited.

"Well, yeah." Wanza finally sparked. "When somebody's paid the price for you, they certainly have rights over you. So, yes, I really believe that, now."

"Since you've confessed it with your mouth and believe it in your heart, Sister Wanza, you are saved."

Wanza drew back and gave the preacher a long, startled stare. "Simple as that?" she said.

"Simple as that." Pastor Meadows confirmed. "So the only thing left to ask is would you like to join this church so you can study the Bible with us and grow in the knowledge of our Lord?"

"Me?" Wanza sat up straight. "Be accepted as a member here? But I ain't nobody—"

"Of course, here," Pastor Meadows said. "We joyfully accept every believer." He gave her a warm smile. "And believe me, Wanza, it's the same for all of us. We come to the Lord feeling so unworthy—but that's why we come—and then He saves us for putting our trust in Him. And then we begin to study His Word together and try to get the hang of this Kingdom-living business."

"Well, then, I guess so." A smile crept over Wanza's solemn face. "Why not?"

"Why not, indeed, Sister Wanza?" Pastor Meadows stepped around his desk and cranked both of her hands. "Talk to my wife on the way out and set-up a day for your baptism."

"Wow! Thank you, Pastor Meadows." Wanza's dull, brown eyes gained new luster. "Me—saved—and a member at True Vine Ministries, Inc. Whatcha know 'bout that!"

CHAPTER 7
Gold Weight

After church the next Sunday, smoke was coming out of Wanza's ears as she drove Yteesha and the kids home in a bright blue haze of rekindled anger. In her rage, she missed her turn and ended up taking a mini-tour of the regal estates in her neighborhood—each one a veritable marvel in brick and mortar of all descriptions. It was a splendid day in May; the kind only Nashville can produce. The sun was bright and shimmering, and the attending breeze was warm and inviting. The rolling lawns that surrounded each of the sprawling mansions looked as if someone— last name *Scissorhands*—had manicured them to exacting standards of perfection.

When they landed on Peacock Place, three streets over, Yteesha lowered her window and stuck out her head. "Miss Wanza! Miss Wanza!" She pointed. "I think that's where Willamina Redd lives. See…all them bushes, there, shaped like guitars." But when Yteesha realized no amount of coaxing could brighten Wanza's dark mood, she buzzed up her window, again, and sat in silence for the remainder of the drive.

When she finally slid her white Escalade into her six-car garage on Legend's Way, Wanza got out and slammed her door with a bang. Yteesha trailed her into the house with the three boys hanging close to her side. They'd also gotten a whiff of the foul mood in the air, and they wanted none of it. Wanza slammed her keys onto the shiny granite countertop in her custom, stainless-steel kitchen. The boys scattered to their rooms, dragging little Austin along with them.

Yteesha let Wanza take a seat on one of the plush, leather stools at the counter before she chanced to speak. "What's the matter, Miss Wanza?"

"The matter?" Wanza seethed. "Did you see how that woman cut her eyes at me all through the service this morning? She has no right to do that. I'm a member there, too!"

"Who?" Yteesha frowned. "Mr. Douglas' new wife?"

"Who else!" Wanza shrieked. "I'm gonna snatch her black hair out by the roots before this is over with."

Yteesha eased her big belly down onto the matching bar stool beside her. "But I don't understand," she said quietly, "why you let that woman make you so mad?"

"What?" Wanza bristled. "That woman stole my husband, and I'm sitting up in church with her every Sunday. The least she could do is apologize!"

"But you got everything she got." Yteesha looked around the beautifully-appointed open floor plan with its airy palette of water blues and sunset oranges. Of course, she'd been introduced to the homes of the rich-and-famous on network reality shows, and they'd scratched her lustful itch as intended. But never in a million years did she think she'd ever know someone who lived in one, or get the chance to stretch out in one herself. "You got this big ole house and fine car." Y ticked off her wish list. "You don't gotta work; he gotta give you child support money; you got his kids—his only kids." Yteesha took a deep breath. "That man's gotta take care o' you, Miss Wanza…no matter where he lay his head at night."

"Is that how you see it?" Wanza's feathers ruffled. "Really?"

"Sure." Yteesha set her elbows on the gleaming counter. "My Mama's name was Yolanda Lee; had me when she was 15. She named me Yteesha Sereeta Lee so my initials would be *YSL* after some whack designer purse she couldn't even afford to buy." She pouted. "And I guess you can tell she had a thing for double-ee's— even named her crack pipe, Willee. Yeah, and Willee took her butt up outta here, too."

"Oh, I'm so sorry to hear that, Yteesha." Wanza calmed.

"I told you to call me 'Y'." She pounded her hand against her short, straight hair; the new growth was starting to itch. "Everybody calls me Y."

"I'm so sorry, Y." Wanza repeated. "Real sorry."

"No worries," Y muttered. "I didn't really know my Mama all that well. My Granny raised me."

"Oh, I see—"

"And when my Mama and my Granny died—the same month—I took up with Charlie Mack." Y tooted her lips. "He'd been sniffing around me, anyhow. And he said he'd take care o' me so I wouldn't have to go into the system. I was just 15."

"So did you get married?" Wanza quizzed.

"No." Y's brows arched in surprise. "Never came up. We lived together. He paid my way. That's how it was."

"So what happened?" Wanza was all ears, now.

"I messed around and got pregnant with Austin when I was 18." Y sighed. "And by that time, Charlie Mack was deep into The Jefferson Street Gang, and he and his boys got popped for doing a drive-by on some members of The Latino Mob, which was trying to move in on their turf. They killed one or two of 'em." She shrugged. "Charlie Mack got sent up for life in the State Pen."

"What did you do then?"

"I didn't know what to do; hadn't never done nothing." Y admitted. "So I took up with Larry Blow, one of Charlie's boys. They'd let him slide 'cause he wasn't in on the drive-by." Y slowly shook her head. "But Larry told me from day-one, he didn't want no kids. He said he didn't even want Austin, but since we was a package deal, he'd have to put up with him."

"Did he mistreat Austin?"

"No." Y defended. "He paid our way. He took good care o' us. But he just kept his distance away from Austin."

"And then—"

"I had to go and get pregnant." Y's head drooped. "And all bets was off." She gripped both sides of her belly. "He beat me so bad I thought I might lose this baby, and then he tossed me and Austin out in the night. He let me have his old car 'cause he said it was a piece of crap just like me, and he wanted to be shed of both of us."

"So where did you go?"

"Didn't have nowhere to go. I had stashed away a few hundred dollars in my jeans that Larry didn't know nothing about. Me and Austin ate fast food and slept in the car." Y whined, jiggling her line and wiggling her bait. "Until that Sunday we ran outta gas and money right in front o' yo' church." She slid her eyes over to Wanza to gauge her reaction to her sob story, and she liked what she saw—another sucker on the line, primed and ready to take care of her. So she set the hook and reeled her in. "Guess it was God's will, huh?"

"No doubt." Wanza agreed heartily. "No doubt." Y's devastating story, tacked onto her own long-line of disappointments, was enough to eat up her insides; gouging them out, again, like reopening an old wound.

Mission accomplished, Y let out a wide, gapping yawn and clambered down off the bar stool. The body-hugging mattress and white down comforter on the king-sized bed in her guest room were calling her name. "I'm sleepy," she said and strolled off to take a nap.

Wanza kicked off her heels and washed her hands to start dinner. *I'm saved, now. So I guess it's my job to help Y.* But, then, when she contemplated the enormity of the task, she sagged against the kitchen sink. And when she considered the universe of dashed hopes and unrealized dreams that they both shared, her frustrated tears mingled in with her cornbread batter.

CHAPTER 8
Golden Rule

"Good morning, Pastor. I see your wife is looking as foxy as ever." Douglas Grand floated into Pastor Meadows' study like a cool summer breeze, sporting a silk gabardine suit with matching tan loafers, sans socks. Every hair on his wavy, black head was meticulously groomed, and his sideburns and moustache were trimmed to perfection. It was his practice to look his best because he toiled under the notion that good looks, a smooth tongue, and the right connections could get you anywhere. "Glad to get your call." Douglas removed his designer, aviator sunglasses and draped his long, lean frame across one of the guest chairs in front of the pastor's desk. "We haven't taken time for a sit-down in forever."

"True." Pastor Meadows responded amiably, sitting behind his desk. He'd brought some order to the clutter in preparation for this meeting. In sharp contrast to Douglas, however, Pastor Meadows had a smooth, round dome, no neck, and square shoulders on a tight, squat frame. He'd grown up in North Nashville and attended Pearl High School. And although he'd walked on the wild side with The Jefferson Street Gang in his youth, he'd rebounded in time to earn a full scholarship to Fisk University—one of the most prestigious, historically black institutions in the nation. Fisk was located right down the sidewalk from his old life, but it opened up a whole new world for Clarence Meadows—a world filled with a wealth of experiences and opportunities beyond his wildest dreams. On a dare, he'd majored in Religion and met his wife, Candi. And during the course of his four years at Fisk, he'd survived all the public school-private school-in the 'hood politics to be there, stay there, and graduate Cum Laude. Pastor Meadows went on to earn a Doctorate of Theology from nearby Belmont University before founding True

Vine Ministries, Inc. When he founded the church at 40, he'd had a full head of black hair. But 10 years later, he'd traded in his few remaining strands of gray for a slick dome. His bushy, black eyebrows were all that remained.

"So...I understand you've been flying all over the globe, Douglas." The pastor proffered.

"Well, I have been pretty busy." Douglas' deep voice rolled like waves against a distant shore. "I'm going international with my business, you know. And these first few months have been critical—have to make the right connections, make some key decisions, build the right foundation—"

"I understand." The pastor nodded in agreement. "A firm foundation is always critical to success."

"True." Douglas crowed. "And it's taking a lot of hard work for me to make that happen—"

"But there's something I need to discuss with you, Douglas." The pastor's voice took on a decidedly serious note. "And I hope you can take the time to walk me through it."

"Whoa!" Douglas' forehead furrowed. "Sounds pretty serious, Pastor. Is the church in some kind of trouble?"

"No." The pastor clarified. "Nothing like that. This is more of a...personal matter."

"Okay." Douglas resituated himself in his chair, fully attentive.

"We have a new member in our congregation." Pastor Meadows interlaced his thick, stubby fingers, set them under his square chin and peered directly into Douglas' eyes.

"Oh?" Douglas squirmed.

"Yes," Pastor Meadows said. "Wanza Johnson-Grand."

"Oh!" Douglas chair squeaked as he shifted, again. But this time, it was to avoid the pastor's intense stare. "Is that right?"

"Yes, Douglas." The pastor's bushy brows leveled into a single, straight line. "And I need your explanation as to why I never knew your wife existed?"

"Well, you see, Pastor." Douglas shifted, again. "You didn't know because Wanza is a very difficult woman. And she refused— flat refused—to attend church…any church. And she refused to let my sons attend with me."

"Is that so?"

"Yes." Douglas flustered. "And as you can imagine, that created irreconcilable differences between us in my home. It was unbearable, just unbearable."

"I can imagine," the pastor said intentionally. "But you never let us know you were married when you joined the church, or when you took over the duties as Chairman of the Finance Committee—"

"Just never came up." Douglas planted his tongue deeply into his handsome jaw.

"And when you decided to take the action to divorce your wife of…"

"Fifteen years." Douglas provided.

"Fifteen years!" The pastor's black brows stood at attention. "Why didn't you bring it to the Deacon Board, or to me? Why didn't you seek counseling to make every attempt to salvage your marriage and your family?"

"But I—"

"You're an officer in this church." Pastor Meadows sizzled like a hot plate under a thick roux. "And as such, we are held to a higher standard. We're expected to be transparent, true and honest with each other…and with this congregation."

"But—"

"Not sharing with us that you had a wife and a family that you'd dumped—"

"Dumped?"

50

"Yes, dumped!" Pastor Meadows stormed. "And asking me, of all people, to marry you and your new wife in our main sanctuary—without telling me—is tantamount to a lie."

"But I—"

"And you made me complicit in that lie by not giving me all the facts and letting me decide how we should proceed, if at all." The pastor blistered.

"But Pastor, since you'd never met Wanza and she wasn't a member here, I didn't think our divorce was any of the church's concern." Douglas' raspy voice grumbled.

"What?" Pastor Meadows' eyes twirled in exasperation, and his bushy brows threatened to pop off in amazement. "Everything that goes on at this church, particularly among our leadership team, is of the utmost importance to me and True Vine!" He was bouncing in his chair, now, finding it difficult to remain seated. "We're building a ministry here based on Biblical principles and what we do and how we do it matters, if we're going to build love and trust among our membership." He gazed across his desk as though he were staring into the face of an absolute stranger. "As leaders, Douglas, it's our responsibility to set a good example. You should know that—"

"I hear you, Pastor." Douglas' nostrils flared, trying to disguise the heat growing under his own collar. "But I have my own life to lead, and I have to do what's good for me. You're building a church. I'm building a business, and I need people on my team who're an asset and not a liability—"

"Your family is not a part of your business plan, Douglas Grand." Pastor Meadows blew. "You have a covenant relationship with your wife—a lifetime commitment!"

"And if I'd stayed with Wanza, I guarantee you one of us wouldn't have made it out alive!" Douglas blared. "When I met Wanza, she was short, shapely and sassy. But, now, she's just short, fat and nasty!"

"I've met Wanza." Pastor Meadows managed to concede the point. "And I'll admit she can be quite a handful—"

"Like I said!" Douglas bristled, feeling exonerated.

"I grant you, she's a lot of bluster and bluff on the outside," the pastor repeated, "but I think she has a real good heart—"

"Think what you will!" Douglas knifed in his point. "But I know the woman!"

"And none of that obviates the fact that you passed yourself off to me, and this leadership team, as a single man." Pastor Meadows searched Douglas' darkening eyes for understanding. "If we had known your marriage was in trouble, we would've tried to help you in every way. You could've gotten counseling, gone through the process of reconciliation—"

"That wasn't gonna happen!" Douglas' eyes flamed.

"So instead," Pastor Meadows said, fuming, "you let me marry you and Melissa with the false impression that she was your one and only bride!"

"Tough!" Douglas' temper finally blew its gasket. "The deed is done! I don't understand why we're having this conversation!"

"And that's the problem in a nutshell, Douglas!" The pastor retorted in kind. "You don't understand! You don't understand that a church leader has to be of the highest moral standards in order to serve the Lord's people—"

"I have a Business degree from Tennessee State University and a Master's in Finance from Vanderbilt University, two of the finest academic institutions in this city." Douglas blared. "And I have more professional experience on my sheet than all of your so-called leadership team combined." His roaring voice was sucking in wind like a jet engine. "I automated the church's finances; oversee its investments; and I've built a business plan that has set you on a course for success." Douglas flamed. "And I challenge you to tell me who has brought in any more lucrative members than me, just from my client list in the music industry alone. Who? Who?"

"Nobody." Pastor Meadows leaned back in his chair, sized-up Douglas, and found him wanting in the balances. "And if you think money is the issue, here," he said evenly, "then things are worse than I suspected." He stared at Douglas across his cluttered desk. "And we have nothing further to discuss."

"Good!" Douglas said, declaring himself the victor in their war of wills.

"And you can leave all of your keys and your access cards with my *foxy* wife on your way out," Pastor Meadows said, squaring his massive shoulders and rising from his desk like an ominous, dark cloud. "Because your services are no longer needed as Chairman of the Finance Committee of True Vine—"

"What?" Douglas howled like a scolded dog. "What're you saying, Man? You can't sit me down!" He jumped up from his chair; slammed his hands down on the desk; and glowered into the pastor's face. "Do you know how much I tithe in this joint—me, not to mention Melissa?" Douglas gnashed his teeth. "Do you know how much my musician friends fork over to you and this church every year? Do you know—"

"I know!" Pastor Meadows rounded his desk, clearly head-and-shoulders shorter than Douglas, and cut him off like a gale-forced wind. "And I know this, too!" He blew. "You can't lead God's people, if you can't serve God's people. And you can't serve them without integrity!"

"Man, you don't know who you're messing with!" Douglas' face pulsed like the brightest bulb in the red-light district. "I can take my wife and blow this joint in a heartbeat—"

"And whether or not you and Melissa stay, I'll leave that to your own discretion." Pastor Meadows locked down on the look of amazement that was registering on Douglas' face, figuring this was his first loss since the playground. "But right this minute," the pastor bellowed, "you'd better leave my office the way you came in—"

"You don't tell me—"

"Or I'll throw you outta here, Mister—head first!" Pastor Meadows' face scrolled to a dangerous shade of green and his hard frame bulked up like The Hulk's. His brows splayed wildly, like he was the reincarnation of the *Jeff* he'd once been in his old, street-gang life. And wisely, Douglas made a speedy escape, having suddenly come to the realization that discretion, most certainly, is the better part of valor.

CHAPTER 9
Gold-Plated

"I had a talk with Pastor the other day," Douglas said casually, while kicking off his loafers in his huge, walk-in closet. It bordered their lavish bed chamber on one side, and Melissa's closet, which was twice its size, flanked it on the other. He flopped down on the French brocade chaise lounge as though he were straining under the weight of the world. "Whew!" He blew out a tired whistle. "I'm stepping down as Chairman of the Finance Committee—"

"You're what?" Melissa's eyes bobbled, trying to figure out her next counter-move to curtail his foolhardiness. "Without talking it over with me?" She flapped. "Why would you do a thing like that?"

Douglas shrugged. "Frankly, Melissa, I'm too busy to do the job justice right now. What with me going international, it's just too much." He stole a peek at Melissa to see how well his story was selling.

"But—"

"I've got to focus, now, more than ever; select good staff; make sure everything is synchronized and running in tip-top shape."

"But I thought Lucas was helping you with all that."

"Lucas is the best right arm I've ever had." Douglas admitted. "But I still have to keep my head in the game and have the final say on all the key decisions."

"This doesn't have anything to do with Wanza, does it?" Melissa pinned him with her prettiest stare.

"Wh-at?" Douglas stammered, seemingly caught off guard. "Not at all." He rose to his feet to avoid her intense gaze. "Why would Wanza have anything to do with my business affairs?"

"She's a member at True Vine, now—"

"In fact, I'd been thinking about us taking a hiatus from True Vine, all together." Douglas angled. "But I know how much you like it there."

"But Douglas, it's the most influential church in Nashville," Melissa said, grasping at straws. "It's a place where you can cut some lucrative deals; meet some powerful people. We can't leave."

Douglas stepped toward her and placed both of her hands in his. "But if we're going to focus on starting a family, Babe," he schmoozed, "I've got to cut back somewhere; haven't I? You're the one who keeps telling me you want kids—"

"Oh, I do, Douglas." Melissa flung her arms around his neck. "I want a house full of kids—"

"And that means more *we* time; right?" He nibbled on her ear.

"Oh, yes." Melissa melted into his arms. "And if stepping down from the chairmanship means I get to spend more nights alone with my husband, well…okay, Babe, I'm all for it."

"I thought that might make you see things my way," Douglas said, enjoying a self-satisfied smirk behind her back.

"But we are staying at True Vine; right?" Melissa recapped.

"Okay, if that's what you want." Douglas agreed. "For now."

"Why, for now?" Melissa pushed back so she could look into his eyes.

"I want to show the pastor my continued support." Douglas lied, without skipping a beat. "And I don't want to uproot my clients who're members there. I can't afford to get them in an uproar when I have so many other irons in the fire," he said, more truthfully. "And…I'm seriously considering going Country."

"Oh?" Melissa puzzled.

"Why not?" Douglas pitched his plan. "I promote young artists from nearly every music genre. Country, you might say, is my final frontier." He grinned at his own pun. "And one of Country's finest just happens to be a new member at True Vine—"

"Willamina Redd?" Melissa chirped.

"Willamina Redd." Douglas' voice dropped into low gear, and the very mention of the woman's name sent visions of her loveliness surging throughout his entire being. Remaining at True Vine and giving Pastor Meadows the satisfaction of thinking he'd won their grudge match was fairly grating on Douglas' nerves. But it was a small price to pay to give his eyes the privilege of scouring the congregation every Sunday morning to indulge in a taste of pretty Miss Redd. *Um-hmm...the sweetest eye-candy on the planet!* And at the thought of her, Douglas turned away from Melissa so she wouldn't feel the quickening of his heartbeat and the thickening of his manly desire for another woman.

CHAPTER 10
Gold Trinket

"Uh-h...hey there, Missy." Money stammered over his pay-by-the-minute cellphone. "Got a minute for yo' Ace?"

"I answered, didn't I?" Melissa's voice crackled over the bluetooth in her bright red Lexus. "I could've let it go to voice mail." She buzzed. "It's because of skimmers and schemers like you that I've had a real hard day at the IRS."

"Ha-Ha." Money chewed on his toothpick. "Tried to wait 'til you got off work and when that man o' yours wasn't around—"

"So...let's have it." Melissa's voice smiled. "What do you want, Big Brother?"

"Well," Money said, "I could use a little advance."

"Advance on what?" Melissa stuck it to him. "Your janitor's wages?"

"Okay, Missy." Money scolded. "I'm serious, here."

"And I'm listening," Melissa said, "so out with it—"

"Well, you see." Money flicked his toothpick from side to side. "I need a little car—"

"Car?" Melissa nearly shouted.

"Yeah," Money said smoothly. "Nothing fancy; just a lil' hoopty so I can get around. My buddy's getting tired o' hauling me, and I'm getting sick o' his mouth."

"Why am I not surprised?" Melissa muttered under her breath. She'd figured their friendship wasn't long for this world. Sooner or later, her brother was usually envied by most of the men in his circle because he was so highly favored by most of the women.

"What's that you say?" Money nudged.

"Oh, nothing." Melissa giggled. "Just giving you a hard time."

"Yeah, I know." Money grinned. "So whatcha say? Got a few duckets for your ole-bro to get him some wheels."

"Sure." Melissa tightened down on her steering wheel. "How much do you need?"

"Uh-h." Money wavered. "Well, you see, I was thinking in the neighborhood of…five thousand—"

"Five thousand dollars?" Melissa flared. "That's a pretty big neighborhood—"

"I know." Money defended. "But it's not all for the car, Missy. I gotta get inspections, insurance, license…stuff like that."

"You're right." Melissa admitted grudgingly. "If you get a car, even dirt cheap, there's a lot that goes along with it."

"So—"

"Okay, Money." Melissa hesitated. "But this is going to wipe out my little secret stash, so this has got to be it for a while. I don't want to have to dip into my joint account with Douglas. If I do, I'll have some 'xplaining to do." She teased. "And that wouldn't be good—for either of us. Understand?"

"Sure, Missy, I get it." Money groused. "So when can I get the cash?"

"Oh, I didn't tell you, did I?" Melissa's voice smiled as she recalled their previous conversation. "Just so you'd never have to step foot in my 'painted pony', again," she said, "I had a secret compartment built into one of those 'big ole columns out there on my big ole front porch.'"

"You did?" Money's toothpick stilled.

"See, I've been looking out for you," Melissa said proudly. "After the last time you were there, I called the carpenter—while Douglas was away on business, of course—and he put in a hidden compartment just as pretty as you please. It's in the column on the right side of the stairs, and it's quite invisible to the naked eye. You just have to put a little pressure on the secret door, and voilà, it pops right open."

"How did you come up with such a bright idea?" Money quizzed.

"Don't you remember?" Melissa exclaimed. "We had a secret door at our house when we were kids."

"Sure did." Money recalled. "It was the door to that little closet under the stairs."

"Yes, and Mother and Daddy never knew because they thought the key was lost—"

"But we found the key," Money said mischievously, "and we used it."

"It was our hiding place when Mother went on a rampage with Daddy—"

"Yes, Lawd!" Money exclaimed. "Mother could play that quiet and humble role at the church-house, having them folk think we were some kind o' perfect family." Money bristled. "But when that woman got to our house, she could call Daddy some names I won't even repeat."

"You're right, Money." Melissa shuttered at the thought.

"Once I overheard Mother telling this woman at church, 'My family is my greatest achievement.'" Money mimicked his mother's prissy tone. "Like we was some kind o' circus-act-in-training, just for her own personal amusement." He ranted. "But we weren't her lab rats. We were people with our own feelings and our own desires—"

"I don't see how Daddy took her abuse all those years." Melissa's brows creased as she strained to keep up with the traffic flashing through her windshield. "But he always knuckled down to her and never said a word."

"Um-hmm." Money mumbled. "Maybe he had good reasons—"

"And if memory serves me right," Melissa said, "you stashed your rum and cigarettes behind our secret door—"

"And I had all kind o' funny cigarettes back then, huh?"

"You sure did." Melissa's voice sterned. "And you'd better not have any, now."

"I don't. I don't." Money swore. "I made you a promise about that, and I'm keeping it."

"No drugs!" Melissa said sternly.

"Scout's honor!" Money's right hand shot up as though she could see him. "None!"

"Ok, then," Melissa said, easing back the throttle and trying to pay better attention to her driving. "I'll put the five thousand dollars in the right column next to the stairs on my front porch. Pick it up when Douglas and I aren't around. And it'll be our little secret…just like old times."

"Yeah." Money tightened down on his toothpick. "Lots of secrets…some you didn't even know—"

"So why didn't you tell me?"

"You liked living in a bubble, Missy." Money jeered. "And I didn't wanna be the one to burst it."

"That's my Money." Melissa sang out sweetly. "Always trying to protect me."

"Besides." Money's voice clouded. "I went off to jail…you went off to college…didn't seem much point back then." He cleared his throat and put the bass back into his voice. "But, maybe, I'll fill you in some day, Missy. You're trying to have your own family, now. So maybe it's time—"

"Why, sure thing." Melissa said with a twinge of sarcasm in her voice. "I'd like nothing better than to hear all about it."

"When?" Money jumped at the chance.

"Suit yourself." Melissa checked the digital clock on her customized, burlwood dash. "But not today, okay." She droned. "It's getting late."

"Yeah, okay." Money agreed. "Ever tell Douglas what it was like growing up—"

"No." Melissa cut him short. "My back-story is my own business."

"Sure thing." Money backed off.

"Your cash will be in our secret stash by tomorrow." Melissa repeated. "Pick it up when Douglas isn't around."

"Have it yo' way, Missy." Money jammed his toothpick between his teeth. "Have it yo' way."

CHAPTER 11
Golden Light

"Well, ladies. Come in. Come in." Pastor Meadows invited Wanza and Yteesha into his study. His desk looked like a cyclone had hit it, as usual. "Take a seat." He offered. "I have some great news."

"Glad to hear it," Wanza said, squeezing herself into the chair at the left of his desk. She dabbed at the sweat pouring from under her red-tipped brunette wig, which was draping over one eye, while wiggling her yellow sundress down over her plump thighs. Yteesha, who couldn't manage more than a loose-fitting smock, eased her heavy load into the chair on the right. "And we've got some good news, too," Wanza said. "And I left a pink box of donuts out there for you and your wife to celebrate. 'Cause this here girl's 'bout to domino."

"Huh?" Pastor Meadows' bushy brows creased in exasperation.

"The baby…she's due in about two weeks." Wanza giggled and squeezed her can of soda onto a leftover fast-food napkin on the corner of his untidy desk. "I tell you if it wasn't for these sodas keeping me cool, I think I'd catch on fire."

"O-kay." Pastor Meadows rubbed the beads of sweat off his slick dome. Wanza always brought more energy into the room than he was prepared to handle. "So you're about to have your baby, Yteesha?" Pastor Meadows consulted her for confirmation.

"Just call me Y, Pastor." She held onto the sides of her enormous belly. "Everybody else does."

"Okay, Y." Pastor Meadows resettled in his chair. "So your baby is due in two weeks, huh?"

"Yes, sir." Y grunted. "The Free Clinic say the baby gonna be due on July 14, 2014."

"Then my news is right on time." The pastor smiled at both women. "We've got you placed at the Women's Services Center on Church Street, over near the Parthenon in Centennial Park. They're expecting you as soon as possible."

"That is good news." Wanza took a swig of her soda. "Although, I will miss Y and my little roomie."

"Yes," the pastor said. "How is little Austin?"

"He fine." Y tried stretching out in her chair with no great success. "Just busy as ever."

"So, Wanza." Pastor Meadows turned to her. "Will you be able to transport Y and little Austin to the Center today or tomorrow?"

"Sure thing, Pastor." Wanza smiled. "In fact, I'll do you one better—"

"What's that?"

"I said it to myself." Wanza explained. "Wherever Y ends up, I'm going over to that place and volunteer—"

"Volunteer?" The other two chimed in.

"Sure." Wanza shrugged. "Wherever you go, you're gonna need help; what with the new baby and all. And I know all them service places need good volunteers. So I'm gonna sign-up, too. I've got the time, 'specially when my boys go back to school in a couple o' months."

"That's admirable, Wanza; I'm sure." The pastor spoke up because Y's mouth was still hanging wide open.

"But I got this!" Y finally spoke up for herself. "I don't need nobody looking over my shoulder."

"But I'm not doing it just for you." Wanza explained. "I'm doing it for me, too."

"But why?"

"I was rambling 'round in that big house all day long, and I was so bored...until you came along, Y. And then I realized I need to help somebody." Wanza turned to Pastor Meadows. "Although, it's been hard 'cause this one, here, won't do nothing." She thumbed over at Y. "Says she's too tired on account o' being pregnant. But, shucks, I held down a full time job, took care of a man and a house when I was pregnant."

"O-kay." Pastor Meadows fumbled, at a loss for words.

"Besides, Pastor," Wanza said, seeking his affirmation, "you've been telling me how I need to get over my anger and bitterness about Doug—"

"Well, something has to give," Pastor Meadows said flatly. "Because my wife has it well documented from some of our members about the shameful behavior that went on in the sanctuary the other Sunday between you and Melissa Grand—"

"But that wasn't my fault!" Wanza screeched; her defenses springing up like the Jericho wall.

"And I don't even know why she be getting all cray-cray over that, Pastor," Y drawled. "She got everything that other woman got. And that man takes care o' her and her kids. So I don't see why she still so mad—"

"O-kay." Pastor Meadows cut her short. He could've kicked himself for taking on these two, feisty women solo. "But more importantly," he said, "it's the Lord's will that we lay our anger and bitterness aside—"

"But, Pastor, you don't know what that man did to me!" Wanza stabbed her finger in Y's direction. "And I keep trying to tell this one, but she don't get it. I never cared about the man's *stuff*. I never wanted his *stuff*. I wanted my man!" She fumed. "I gave him my heart. I gave him my soul. I gave him my life. And he took it...he took it all!" The anger in Wanza's chest was about to explode. "And, then, he hurt me...he hurt me so bad. I lost everything...I lost me! And I want it back! I want it all back—"

"O-kay," Pastor Meadows said quietly, trying to calm the waters.

But Wanza wasn't having it. She was too fired-up to stop. "You see, I was just 23; putting myself through college; waiting tables in the West End at the same time Douglas was finishing up at Vanderbilt." She flamed. "He was more serious than the other guys that came down there wilding it up and passing girls around like party favors. So when Douglas picked me out o' the crowd, I was flattered. I didn't have nothing. I wasn't going nowhere, but Douglas wanted me, anyhow." Wanza breathed. "So I married the man. I quit my job. I dropped out o' Tennessee State. I worked in his office pregnant. I worked in his office with babies on my hip. I worked in his office with babies in a playpen. I worked by his side 24-7—"

"And looks to me like you worked yo'self out of a job." Y stretched her aching back, and Pastor Meadows signaled for her to zip it.

"Go on." He encouraged Wanza. "Go on."

Wanza shot Y a wicked side-eye and continued. "And then he brings me out here to this barren wasteland; away from all I know; and dumps me in some big ole house I don't even want 'cause it made him look good." Wanza boiled. "And then he starts telling me how I don't fit in; starts coming to your church 'cause it made him look good." She sizzled. "And then he takes up with Miss Melissa behind my back 'cause he thinks she makes him look good…better than me." Wanza's rage finally broke down into piercing sobs. "Uggh!" She wept bitterly. "But what about me? What about me?"

"I understand." The pastor's voice stroked consolingly.

"No, you don't!" Wanza flung her red-streaked bangs out of her eyes. "None of you understand…how Douglas left me…after 15 years…after all I did for him!" She wailed. "He left *me*…his ride-or-die…for that skinny, stringy-haired, long-legged—"

"Wanza!" Pastor Meadows broke in before her temper carried her too far.

66

"See, Pastor." Y yawned dispassionately. "She keep crying 'bout the same old thang, and she won't open up her eyes and see she got it made. She got everything any woman could want." Y huffed. "Humph! Wish I was in her shoes...just for one day. I'd be satisfied to let that man take care o' me."

Pastor Meadows passed Wanza a tissue from the blue box on his messy desk and motioned for Y to pipe down. He let things settle a bit before speaking, again. "Wanza," he said consolingly, "I know you've been hurt by the circumstances of your past."

"Uh-huh." She nodded

"But, now, that you're a baptized believer," the pastor said, "you have a choice."

"Huh?" Wanza sniffed.

"You can choose—" Pastor Meadows opened up his big, right hand. "To forgive Douglas—the same way Jesus forgives you." Then he balled the same hand into a tight fist. "Or you can choose— to stay bitter and grow harder—"

"But I don't wanna be hard." Wanza sobered.

"So then you've got to pray through your past and choose to forgive."

"But how?" Wanza sniffled.

"Cry. Scream. Do whatever you need to do to get it all out of you." Pastor Meadows implored. "But tell the truth, the whole truth, and nothing but the truth to Jesus—what Douglas did *and* what you did. And, then, forgive all parties involved...including yourself." Pastor Meadows shook his hands free and turned them both, palms up. "Release it. Let it go." He caught Wanza's eye. "Can you do that?"

"Well...okay." She squirmed. "I'll try."

"And considering your past history with Douglas and Melissa," Pastor Meadows said, sweeting the pot, "on behalf of the church,

I've asked Douglas to step down as Chairman of the Finance Committee—"

"What?" Wanza's dull eyes sparkled as her defenses came tumbling down. "You'd do that…for me?"

"And Douglas has consented." The pastor fudged the truth a bit. "He agrees that since you're a member, now, it's only fair." His eyes pinned her under bushy brows. "So, now, Wanza, I'm asking you," he said, "will you please cut Douglas and Melissa some slack?"

Wanza thoughtfully considered his request. "Okay, Pastor." She blinked. "I'll do it. I'll do it for you. I'll do it for the church. I'll do it for the Lord."

"Whew!" Y let out a loud sigh. "And it's about time!"

CHAPTER 12

Golden Gleam

"Hel-lo." Pastor Meadows struggled to open his eyes and engage his brain to respond to the ringing telephone in his bedroom. "Who is this?" He took a peek at the clock on his bedside table. "It's 3 o'clock in the morning!"

"It's me, Pastor." The voice whispered. "Wanza."

"What is it...this time of morning?" The pastor braced himself for bad news. "What could be so important?"

"I'm at Nashville General," Wanza said excitedly. "And Y just had her baby...it's a girl!"

"Wonderful!" Pastor Meadows sat up in bed, careful not to disturb his wife who was sleeping soundly beside him. "But I thought the baby was due on the 14th. Is everything alright?"

"Well, it's July 4th, and the baby's here—fine and dandy. Just goes to show what these doctors know, huh?" Wanza grumbled. "But she was born about midnight. And I got here about an hour ago, in kind of a rush, when Mrs. Lawson at the Women's Services Center gave me a call." Wanza tugged on her black, flip wig to be sure it was in place. "I had left my name as next of kin, you know. Besides, Mrs. Lawson knows me 'cause I volunteer three times a week over at the Center."

"So you went ahead with that," Pastor Meadows said, "volunteering, I mean?"

"Well, yeah." Wanza smarted. "I told y'all I needed something to do. Besides, they didn't assign me to Y's case, at all. They stuck me right in the front office when they found out I have a background in business. They desperately needed somebody to help them out with the books. And you know I used to do the accounting for Douglas when he first got started."

"And you're okay with that?"

"It's alright for now," Wanza said, "and it gives me a chance to keep an eye on Y and Austin. You know I want the best for that little boy."

"And how's that working out?" Pastor Meadows whispered.

"Uh-h." Wanza hesitated. "Hard to tell right now," she said. "They tell me Y won't do nothing for herself or Austin; says she's too tired to go to school or help out in the nursery."

"But maybe that'll change since she's had the baby?"

"Maybe, but I've seen women like Y before. They want all they can get without doing anything in return." Wanza breathed. "But I sure do hope I'm wrong."

"I hope you're wrong, too." Pastor Meadows yawned. "Because that kind of behavior won't go over too well at the Center. They have requirements, you know; and they make them stick."

"I'm figuring that out by working in the front office." Wanza giggled. "Them little ladies ain't no joke. They expect those girls to pull themselves up by their boot straps…or else."

"Something like that." Pastor Meadows eked out a chuckle. "But anyway, I'm glad you could be there for Y tonight."

"You know what she named the baby, Pastor?"

"No. What?"

"Teesha Ynaee!" Wanza steamed. "Wasn't it bad enough her mama saddled her with them double-ee's? Why would she go 'head and pass the madness down to her kids?" Wanza rustled like a mother hen. "But they ain't naming these kids no mo', Pastor. They're marking 'em for all the world to see—*black-baby-no-daddy.*"

"I hear you, Wanza." Pastor Meadows squeezed back a pained chuckle. "I'd better go before I wake up Candi, and that won't be pretty. You have a good night and take good care of yourself."

"Who was that?" Candi Meadows turned and patted her husband's broad back.

"Wanza," Pastor Meadows whispered. "Yteesha Lee had her baby tonight—a girl."

"I've been dreaming about those two ladies." Candi yawned. "I've been praying for them, too…them and their kids."

"Good, Honey." Pastor Meadows snuggled his mass back under his wife's warm body and kissed her neck. "Very good."

CHAPTER 13

Gold Fleck

"Babe, I've been thinking," Douglas said to Melissa, across the cozy candlelight at their special table at Chez Jacques in celebration of their first anniversary. It was a cool evening in October. The restaurant's open-hearth fireplace was crackling happily in one corner, and they were decked out in their finest silks and leathers. Douglas had already treated Melissa to a new set of five-carat diamond bangles and the blissful surprise of white-gloved waiters carting in a flaming cake in their honor.

"Hmm." Melissa cooed, feeling so very special. "What've you been thinking, Babe?"

Douglas straightened his expensive tie. "I've been thinking of expanding my business plan."

"Really?" Melissa rewarded him with an easy smile.

"To include…you." Douglas waited for her reaction.

"Me?" Melissa's gorgeous eyes widened. "But how can you include me?"

"You're a CPA in a dead-end job over at the IRS—"

"I wouldn't say that." Melissa quickly defended her position. "I have opportunities for advancement. Why, just today my boss was saying—"

"Like I said," Douglas reiterated, not appreciating her interruption. "It's a dead-end job because it belongs to your boss and not to you."

"Well, that's true." Melissa conceded. "But—"

"I want to make you your own boss, Melissa." Douglas beamed at her. "Since I bought that warehouse complex in Printer's Alley, I want to divvy up the space and set you up in your own suite of offices at the new corporate headquarters of Star Music Promotions International."

"But, my dear husband," Melissa said, trying to make light of her deep apprehension, "what could I possibly do for you?"

"There's a lot you can do for me." Douglas ran his socked foot up her bare leg under the draped table.

"Ah-h, Babe!" Melissa exhaled as chills ran up her spine.

"But as it relates to Star," Douglas continued, "some of my younger artists are straight outta the 'hood, Babe. They don't know a thing about handling big money. The music business is all so new to them, and they're surrounded by leeches and bad influences that will eat them alive...and that's bad for business—my business."

"Is that so?" Melissa attempted to focus.

"But they trust me...and they need you." Douglas was all business, now. "They need someone who can help them plan their finances; handle their taxes; set up bank accounts; create workable investment portfolios. Heck, they need somebody to put them on a budget so they don't end up buying five Rolls, three houses, and giving it all away to some conniving homeboy; greedy baby-mama; or their own dysfunctional mamas before they've gotten their feet under their new career."

"I see," Melissa said. Douglas' fire was making her hot as usual. "But wouldn't this be considered a conflict of interest...since I'm your wife?"

"It's a conflict of interest, if I say it's a conflict of interest." Douglas' temples pulsed. He wasn't accustomed to having his ideas batted around and jammed back down his throat. "And besides," he said stiffly, "you'll share my office space and the clients I send your way, but we will not share their confidential information. The left hand won't know what the right hand's doing, so to speak. I won't tell you, and you won't tell me. Understood?"

"I guess that could work." Melissa mulled it over as though she had a choice.

"And it won't be the movers-and-shakers I'll be sending your way." Douglas clarified. "My premiere clients are sophisticated enough to have their own investment advisors and tax consultants," he said. "No. This will be the newbies; those just cutting their teeth on the business and who need some guidance and hand-holding until they break into the bigs." Douglas flashed her a wink to suggest they were on the same team. "And I can trust you to treat them right."

"Wow!" Melissa's voice tensed. "Sounds like a lot of work…and what will you be doing?"

"Me?" Douglas bristled, resenting her questioning his movements. "I'll be doing what I do—growing my client base, expanding my international markets…got a trip to Japan just next month. And I'll be growing my genres. I'm going hard after Country—"

"Is Willamina Redd helping you with that?" Melissa shot him a cautious eye.

Douglas slid his foot back to his side of the table, since the mere mention of woman's name filled him to exploding. He took a sip of wine to dowse the flames and camouflage his lustful intentions. "We've had a few casual discussions…off the record." He admitted dismissively. "She's starting to come around to my way of thinking."

"Oh, I see." Melissa nodded, not totally satisfied with his response. "And what about our family?" Her wide eyes flickered in desperation.

"What about our family?" Douglas' temper was starting to run hot.

"We're trying to get pregnant; remember?" Melissa said softly, attempting to diffuse his growing annoyance. "And with both of us working so hard—"

"You're trying to get pregnant." Douglas stiffened.

"But you said we could start *our* family." Melissa bit her pretty bottom lip. "You know I want a house full of babies—"

"So you've said…on numerous occasions." Douglas' fine nostrils flared.

"It's been over a year, Babe." Melissa cooed. "And nothing's happened, so that's why I've been trying to get you to go see Dr. Barrows with me…so we can find out what's wrong."

"Well, it's obviously not me." Douglas blared. "And I've got two, growing boys to prove it."

"But the tests work best if we see Dr. Barrows together." Melissa pleaded.

"And I told you, I'm not taking any tests from any doctor." Douglas flamed. "I don't have that kind of time." He was struggling to keep his temper under control since some of the classy patrons were starting to take an interest in their heated debate. "I say, if it happens it happens; and if it doesn't, it doesn't." He ground out the words between clenched teeth. "But in the meantime, Melissa, I'm offering you an opportunity to grow your career right alongside mine at Star Music Promotions International."

"I know that." Melissa whined. "But with all the extra work, how will we ever find time to be together—"

"Enough!" Douglas tossed his napkin into his untouched dessert. "Do you want to help me grow my business, Melissa, or not?"

"Of course, I do, Douglas." Melissa cowered, remembering how Wanza had gotten the axe when she'd opposed him. And, now, she had herself and Money to consider. She was in no position to play hardball with Douglas Grand, despite the relentless cuckoo gonging out the years on her biological clock—*37, 38…40!*

"Then that settles it." Douglas pushed back from the table, satisfied with the results. He could keep close tabs on his wife at his headquarters building, while having a clear field to make an end-run at Miss Willamina Redd. *And, oh, how my body aches for that woman. It may take a little time and some careful planning to break her down, but I'll move the moon and sky to get to you, Miss Redd.* Douglas sucked his bottom lip like he could already taste the honey. "So, Melissa," he said, sealing the deal with an air of finality, "I'll have your new offices ready for move-in by next week."

"Next week? No two-week notice to the IRS—" Melissa caught a whiff of Douglas' stern eye and caved. "Guess not."

"Check!" Douglas blared at the startled waiter.

CHAPTER 14
Golden Touch

"Hi, Money," Melissa chirped over the bluetooth while cruising her way to the Brentwood Estates. The traffic on I-65 South was thick, and her usual 30-minute drive was turning into a 60-minute nightmare. She was trying, with limited success, to maneuver her Lexus into the far right lane so she wouldn't chance missing her exit in the milieu. "How are you?"

"Peachy." Money bit down on his toothpick and slid out into the alley so he could hear her better. He was working in his building's basement, and the boilers could get a little noisy. "How you be?"

"Just wanted to tell you my news." Melissa worked at sounding chipper.

"Uh-huh." Money swept the soot from his orange janitor's jumpsuit with one hand, while juggling his pre-paid cellphone in the other. "Speak."

"I quit my job today." Melissa's voice trembled.

"You?" Money puzzled. "Ditched the IRS…that good-paying government job? But why?"

"Because I'm going to provide CPA services to some of Douglas' young clients downtown at the new headquarters of Star Music Promotions International." Her voice perked, sounding like a rehearsed commercial.

"Oh?" Money flipped his toothpick to one side. "So…is this good news?"

"Well." Melissa waffled. "I guess it's a bittersweet blessing."

"How so?"

"I get to be closer to Douglas—"

"Just cause you in the joker's office don't mean you'll be no closer to him." Money shot back. "From what I hear, he's all over the place. You're the one who'll be stuck in his office, not him."

"But Money," Melissa whined, "it'll make me more involved in his business affairs. And he wants to help me grow my career—"

"But why he wanna do a thing like that for you? What's in it for him?" Money groused. "Sounds to me like the old shell game—"

"What're you saying?"

"'Look at the shell…don't look at the pea.'" Money shot her a rhyme. "And what pea do you think Douglas might be hiding under his shell, hmm? Could he be giving you the run-around so he can do a li'l running around of his own?"

"Money, you have such a devious mind—"

"You don't graduate Prison U being no wuss." Money snapped back. "And you'd better start opening up your own eyes and ears—"

"But Douglas would never do a thing like that to me." Melissa protested.

"Uh-huh." Money squeezed down on his toothpick. "Are you forgetting how you got him?"

"Well—" Melissa bit her pretty lip, thoughtfully. "Douglas may be working a little too close to Willamina Redd for my liking—"

"Who-dat?"

"She's this new Country superstar." Melissa explained. "You've heard of her. She just won a Grammy for Best New Music Artist of the Year."

"Nope." Money teased. "Not up on my Country."

"Well, you'd better get up on it." Melissa tittered. "You're in Nashville, now—"

"But you can never tell what a man has on his mind, Missy." Money retorted. "'Cause Daddy sure had a pea hiding under his shell." He sniffed. "He had a mistress, you know."

"No!" Melissa's voice spiked, and she nearly nicked the bumper of the car ahead of her. "I don't believe you!"

"Well, he did." Money firmed. "I kept it under wraps to protect you—"

"So why're you telling me this now?" Melissa bristled.

"Just been thinking—" Money's voice broke.

"Just been drinking is more like it." Melissa flared.

"You said you wanted to know some things." Money reminded her. "Besides, I gotta start getting this stuff off my chest. Don't want it to land me back in prison, again—"

"So tell me—"

"Remember that time…Deacon Ragland put his hands on you?" Money's voice clouded.

"What?" Melissa braked suddenly, trying to catch up with her brother's rapid train of thought. "That was a long time ago, Money. I was only…14."

"And Daddy was sitting right there; remember?" Money grumbled. "He had to see what I saw when I walked into his office and yelled, 'Hey, you! Get your stinking hands off Missy!'"

"Yes." Melissa gripped onto her steering wheel. "And Deacon Ragland was so shocked he nearly tripped over you running out of there, too. But Daddy said, 'Now, Son, you're way out of line.' She mimicked his anemic tone, which was a cross between a flickering light bulb and a sputtering engine. "And he made you go and apologize to Deacon Ragland—"

"But I was so mad when I walked out o' there." Money seethed afresh. "It must o' been all over me, too, 'cause Mother Whatnot rolled up on me in the hallway—"

"And I bet you smelled her coming looong before you saw her, huh?" Melissa snickered. "She always smelled like that liniment she used for her 'arthur-ritis', and she always tried to cover it up with that cheap, dollar-store perfume. Pee-ew!"

"Pee-ew is right!" Money snorted.

"So what did that old, self-professed *prayer warrior* have to say?" Melissa jeered.

"Well, she caught me by the elbow and said, 'Some church folk give church a bad name, Son. Everybody at church ain't in church. Some of 'em just be making an outside show to the world." Then she laid one of her li'l gnarly hands on me and said, "But you've got a good heart, Son. So don't you let none o' these folk turn you around; you hear me. You read yo' Bible. And you get to know Jesus for yo'self.'"

"And what did you say to that?" Melissa puzzled.

"Nothing. I just shook her off and kept stepping. But I wasn't wrong, was I Missy? I wasn't wrong? Was I?" Money prodded her like a nagging child. "Didn't that man put his hands on you?"

"You were right, Money." Melissa's hands tensed on the steering wheel, and she struggled to focus on the car ahead of her. "And that wasn't the first time he'd tried to feel on me, either. But since Daddy wouldn't let us say bad things about Deacon Ragland or anybody else at church, I didn't know what to do—"

"I knew I was right!" Money exclaimed, like he was breaking loose from years of hypocrisy.

"I was too much of a coward to ask you back then." Melissa admitted sheepishly. "But did you ever apologize to Deacon Ragland?"

"No way!" Money snorted. "That's the day I decided Daddy was worthless, and I'd have to look out for you myself." He fumed like it was yesterday. "So I marched right into Ragland's office and said, 'If you ever put your hands on Missy, again, I'm gonna call your wife; and, then, we'll see what's what!'"

"And what did he say?"

"He laughed right in my face." Money growled. "He said, 'Boy, you're only16 years old, and you don't know who you're messing with! You can play this goodie-two-shoes act around here if you want to, but I'll put it out that you ain't nothing but a two-bit hoodlum-in-the-making, and nobody'll believe a word you say.' And then he cocked his crooked mouth to one side and said, 'And before you go calling anybody's wife, you'd better ask your Daddy what he does on Tuesday nights.'"

"What did he mean by that?" Melissa rumbled.

"Didn't know at the time." Money checked his temper. "But that next Tuesday night, when Mother went to bed early, I snuck out and followed Daddy."

"That's right." Melissa recalled. "Mother always went to bed early on Tuesday nights."

"And you know what I saw?" Money said, grinding his toothpick between clenched teeth.

"What?"

"Daddy was at Sister Sistrunk's house." He croaked. "I peeked in through her window. They were drinking and laughing…grinding and kissing—"

"No!" Melissa's mouth dropped open. Of course, she remembered Miss Pearly Sistrunk. She was this prim, sturdy-looking, middle-aged woman who worked at the library. She always sat on the row directly behind her mother, trying to out-do her big hats. "So what did you do?"

"I was so mad. I went a little nutty-brained." Money's anger refueled. "That's the night I went next door to Mr. Solomon's house. I snatched down every pear off his prized trees." Money's voice spiked with every word. "And with every pear, I kept saying, 'Them-Lying-Cheating-Church-Playing Hypocrites!'"

"Oh, so that *was* you?" Melissa twittered. "Poor Mr. Solomon came over the next day asking Mother if you'd done it—"

"And what did she say?" Money growled.

"She said, "One of Pastor Mann's children would never do such a thing. And if you persist in this line of inquiry, I will surely have no recourse than to take it up with the Pastor!'" Melissa parroted her mother's prissy tone with its razor-sharp edge.

"Bet that scared the bejeebers out the po' man." Money chuckled. "Mother had Daddy's rep built pretty high back in those days."

"Yes, indeed." Melissa snickered. "Mr. Solomon backed off, alright. But I guess that's why he built his privacy fence a little bit higher and never spoke a single word to any of us, again."

"Wish I could say the same for Pearly Sistrunk." Money grunted.

"And, you know, she probably sat behind Mother every Sunday so no one would notice when Daddy's roving eyes floated over in that hussy's direction—"

"Hold on!" Money interrupted her tirade. "Better watch how you slang them kind o' words around, Missy."

"What? Hussy?" Melissa flared. "Well, she was a hussy—sleeping around with another woman's husband—"

"Like I said." Money snickered.

"Oh!" Melissa's voice blushed. "But, no, there was more to it between me and Douglas…really—"

"So then—" Money said, easing his sister off the hook and exiting his painful past as quickly as he'd revisited it. "Just how are you and Mrs. Wanza Johnson-Grand getting along these days?"

"Huh?" Melissa slowed to make her exit and to negotiate the sharp turns in her brother's mind. "Well, she's getting a little better, actually. She doesn't glare at me through the entire service anymore. And she's stopped dressing like she's from planet Mars."

"Guess you've gotta take your blessings where you find 'em, huh—mixed or otherwise." Money took a parting shot at Douglas' role in forcing his sister to quit her good IRS job.

"And how's your new car working out?" Melissa shot right back. "Hope you spent my money wisely."

"I'd say you made a wise investment." Money snorted.

"How so?" Melissa played along.

"I did a Wanza drive-by in my new hoopty just the other night."

"You did?"

"Told you'd I'd keep an eye on the situation." Money nodded coolly. "'Cause if this thing between you and Wanza ever becomes more than a spittin' contest, I'm prepared to take it to another level—"

"So what did you find out?"

"Seems like the pregnant girl is gone for good and all is quiet on her end of your street."

"Well, I should've figured Wanza was up to something." Melissa sniped. "She makes this big show of helping the girl so the church would be solidly behind her when it came out that she's Douglas' ex-wife. And now that she's made her grandstand play, I guess she's kicked that girl back into the streets where she belongs."

"And how's that working out for you?" Money twirled his toothpick.

"Oh, I see some of the women at church cutting their eyes at me like I'm the witch that stole Douglas from that *nice-Miss-Wanza*." Melissa sniffed. "But that just makes me hold my head up that much higher. After all, I'm the one and only, Mrs. Douglas Grand."

"You go, Girl!" Money snickered. "You really are your mother's daughter."

CHAPTER 15
Gold-Studded

The Monday after the calendars had turned over on New Year's Day, Douglas summoned Melissa into his office for an emergency meeting at 10 a.m. sharp. His executive office was an eclectic mix of chrome with red and black leathers. When Melissa arrived, on time, he had his back to her gazing at his star-studded wall of famous photos, platinum records and stellar awards. The scent of greed and raw ambition clouded the room like a heavy waft of smoke from an imported cigar.

"You see this wall, Melissa," Douglas said without turning to greet her. "This wall represents my clients' astronomical success in the music business. And by association as their promoter, it represents my accomplishments, as well."

"I know that, Douglas." Melissa stood planted at the door, unsure of what to do next. "Turn around and look at me," she said, happy she'd chosen to look her stunning best this morning. Her hair was dark and sleek, makeup flawless, and the few pounds she'd lost put her long legs on full display in her short Armani skirt and five-inch, Louboutin red-bottom heels.

Douglas turned slowly and eyed her up and down. "Looking mighty tasty this morning, Mrs. Grand," he said. "Take a seat."

Bolstered by his compliment, Melissa slid into one of the red chrome side chairs and gave him her brightest smile. "You asked to see me." She beamed.

"Lil Dee said you dissed him." Douglas launched in without preamble, taking a seat in his high-back leather chair behind his masterful desk of chrome and glass. "He said, and I quote, 'Now, that Miss Wanza, that lady's straight-up hard; tells it like it be. But she ain't never dissed me like this new female you got hooked up with—Miss Me-Lissa with her turned-down nose and stuck-up ways. What be her problem, anyhoo, Man?'"

"I did not disrespect Lil Dee." Melissa rebutted in her own defense. "I'm just trying to help the guy—"

"These are *my* clients, Melissa, and you are not their den mother." Douglas fumed. "You cannot tell Lil Dee you might be able to understand him better if he takes out his grill!"

"But I couldn't understand a word he was saying—"

"Lil Dee's diamond-encrusted platinum grill is probably worth more than your Lexus!" Douglas shouted. "You get an interpreter if you must, but you do not dis Lil Dee. He's booked in London this month and Tokyo next month. His talent pays for our lifestyle. Show some respect!"

"But his credit score is in the toilet. He can't even get a credit card." Melissa screeched. "And now that he's got plenty of cash, I'm trying to work with him to get his credit repaired—"

"As long as you're in my headquarters, you represent me!" Douglas nailed her to the wall. "Star Financial Enterprises may be your own exclusive, spin-off company, with your own suite of offices, and your own staff; but you're in *my* building, and these are *my* clients. Is that clear!"

"Of course, it's clear." Melissa cowered. "But—"

"Melissa, most of these young artists are from the projects." Douglas continued, uninterrupted. "They didn't even finish high school, not to mention college. These kids are used to getting shafted, ignored, pushed aside, and they feel that very deeply. They feel like they have no one on their side." Douglas lectured. "That's where I come in. I look out for them. I promote them. I make them rich. And in return, they put their trust in me. And I don't need anybody screwing that up!" Douglas flamed out of control. "I cut you some slack in 2014 because you were just getting your feet wet. I even let you slide through the holidays. But you've been here over three months, now, for God's sake. It's a new year. It's 2015! And I've got to move my business forward. I don't have time to be watching my back. And you *cannot* act stuck-up around these kids, Melissa. They're sensitive."

"I'm sorry, Douglas." Melissa slid in on the tiny crack in his anger. She moved over and sat on the edge of his desk. She crossed her sensuous legs and showed off the goods. "But I'm sensitive, too, Babe."

Douglas' hands found her legs and caressed the full length of them. "I know you didn't mean any harm, Babe." He calmed. "But dissing my clients is bad for business."

"I know." Melissa moaned and ran her hot tongue along his cheekbone, kissing him in his ear. "And I'll never let it happen, again." She raised her dainty right palm and the multi-colored diamond bangles he'd given her for their first anniversary tinkled down her slender wrist. "Promise."

"Okay, Babe." Douglas rewarded her with a half-smile.

"What're you doing tonight?" Melissa stoked the flames of the fire.

"Got a meeting." Douglas' jaws tightened.

"With me, I hope," she said, working hard to keep the dying embers alive. "I've got something special planned just for you—"

"Nope. Sorry." Douglas clipped. "Willamina Redd is introducing me to Willie Nealy tonight—"

"*The* Willie Nealy." Melissa feigned excitement in the face of his rejection. "The Country Legend himself?"

"Yep." Douglas preened. "I get a private meet...and a chance to pitch my services."

"Can I go?" Melissa gushed. "I'd love to meet Willie Nealy...just this once."

"No." Douglas shut her down. "I suggest you go home, get some rest and get your act together, Melissa. You seem a bit frazzled."

"But I've been so busy…trying so hard to fit in—"

"And that's my problem, how?" Douglas snapped. "Are you expecting me to change my schedule to help you out? Ha!" He smirked. "Not gonna happen."

"But we need to spend more time together, Douglas."

"Whatever." Douglas flat-lined. "See you at home later. I've got work to do."

CHAPTER 16
Gold Chain

"Money, I'm worried." Melissa's admission vibrated through the bluetooth in her empty Lexus.

"Oh, hey, Missy." Money sang out over his pre-paid tracfone. "Whatzup?"

"Just had a big blow-out with Douglas about one of his clients." Melissa explained.

"Oh?" Money's voice frowned. "So where're you now?"

"In my car!" Melissa hammered her steering wheel. "Headed home!"

"Good." Money chomped down on his toothpick. "What happened?"

"It's been so hard trying to work with these ghetto brats." Melissa's voice bristled. "They don't understand how things work in the real world, and I can't comprehend their ignorant ways half the time. They speak in code, lingo, sign language…something totally indistinguishable."

"Yeah." Money snickered. "Bet it is a culture shock for you, *Miss-Head-of-my-Class-at Vandy*."

"Quit that, Money." Melissa scolded. "I need your support."

"So is that all that's got you so wired?" Money prodded. "Or are you catching grief from Wanza, too?"

"No, I guess Wanza cooled off after the church announced that Douglas resigned his leadership role." Melissa groused. "But I still have to see her at True Vine every Sunday. And she is an unpleasant reminder of what happens to Douglas' wives when they displease him." She faltered. "And she has his kids, Money…and I don't. How can I compete…keep his interest? This whole thing has me feeling like less than a woman—"

"You'll be fine, Missy." Money twirled his toothpick like a swizzle stick. "Just hang in there."

"That's easy for you to say." Melissa steamed. "I'm so stressed out about this baby thing I can hardly concentrate at work. My hair's falling out in clumps. I'm losing weight. And I don't know why—"

"What did the doctors say?"

"They say they can't find anything wrong with me," Melissa babbled. "They say they don't see any reason why I can't get pregnant, but they'd like to examine Douglas, too. But he just refuses to go with me, Money. Flat refuses!"

"The man's busy, Missy."

"Yeah, busy sucking up to Willamina Redd." Melissa fumed. "She just won a Grammy, you know—"

"Is that woman pretty—that Country star, I mean?" Money quizzed.

"I guess you could say she's pretty." Melissa pursed her luscious lips. "She's young. She's white. She's got an amazing figure. She's a redhead."

"Um-hmm…then I'd say be worried!" Money blared. "I wouldn't trust your husband around a pretty, young thang as far as I can throw a fat elephant."

"You're not helping, here, Money." Melissa tensed on her steering wheel.

"Well, I tell it like I see it—"

"And what I see are the hands of my biological clock spinning out of control." Melissa screeched. "I'm nearly 37, Money…and no babies!"

"Tell me about it." Money snickered. "I'm staring 40 dead in the face, and it's like looking down the business-end of a high-powered rifle."

"But it's impossible to get pregnant when your husband's never home." Melissa whined. "And when he is home, he's too tired to move."

"Yep, that can cut down your odds, alright." Money clucked.

"He says he's spending nights at the headquarters trying to catch up. But he had the energy to chew me out in his office today, with his secretary and all those other knuckleheads listening." Melissa steamed. "And he refused to let me join him and Willamina when she introduces him to Willie Nealy later tonight."

"*The* Willie Nealy?" Money whistled. "Willamina's got that kind o' juice?"

"Oh, I thought you didn't speak Country." Melissa sniped.

"Everybody knows Willie Nealy. He's a legend in his own time." Money grumbled. "And Douglas wouldn't let you tag along with him and Miss Redd, huh?"

"No!" She yelped. "Turned me down flat!"

"Well, I wouldn't worry, Missy." Money soothed. "You're the wife. You've staked out your claim. You're holding the purse strings—"

"Speaking of which, Money, do you need anything?" Melissa pouted. "I'm in the mood to spend some of that precious cash that Douglas spends all of his time stockpiling."

"Well...you know me—"

"Tell you what," Melissa said conspiratorially. "I'm going to stash you another five thousand dollars behind our secret door, and you can pick it up when you're ready. But make it last this time, Money...and no funny business—"

"Don't let this stuff make you all nutty-brained, Missy." Money squeezed on his toothpick. "'Cause I've been thinking...that's what sent me to prison the first time."

"What?" Melissa struggled to navigate the sharp turns in her brother's logic.

"Daddy having that mistress—"

"I beg to differ," Melissa said when she'd caught up. "What sent you to prison the first time was you hooking up with those other two fools who wanted to rob Milgrum's Liquor Store. You had a college scholarship just waiting for you, and you did something crazy like that—"

"Yeah, but the first time them two jokers rolled up on me with the idea, I said, 'No.'" Money's voice clouded. "But then I kept sneaking over there, seeing Daddy pawing all over that woman—preaching fire and brimstone on Sundays and cheating with Pearly Sistrunk on Tuesdays. Made me nutty-brained—"

"Do you think Mother knew?"

"Sure, she knew!" Money blared. "She had to know. She had spies all over the church and half the town, trying to keep Daddy locked-in solid as the Senior Pastor; 'specially, since being the First Lady of Faith Freewill was her single claim to fame!"

"You're right." Melissa granted. "She did go to bed early every Tuesday night like clockwork—"

"Yep, so she wouldn't have to face up to what Daddy was doing...and be forced to have to deal with it."

"But why wouldn't Mother let on to us?"

"She wanted you to believe the fairy tale—"

"What fairy tale?"

"The fairy tale that she'd created the perfect family and she had her man in check."

"Maybe." Melissa's foot slipped off the gas. "And maybe, Daddy wasn't such a wimp, after all. Maybe, he was just struggling under a boatload of guilt. He knew Mother knew...and taking her mess was his way of making it up to her." Melissa slowed. "Or maybe, Mother's mess is what drove him into another woman's arms in the first place—"

"Either way," Money said in his cool style, "I didn't have nobody I could talk to 'bout it…nobody I could tell. And holding all that mad inside o' me made me do some crazy things—"

"But you could've told me." Melissa protested.

"I'm telling you, now." Money chomped down on his toothpick. "Just trying to show you how stuff can happen…so you don't go getting all nutty-brained and do something crazy, too."

"So many secrets…so many lies—"

"So, when them two crooks rolled back up on me the second time about that robbery," Money said, sliding back into his story, "I got to thinking. 'What-the-hay? Might as well join the rest of these church-going hypocrites.' So I said, 'Sure thing. I'll do it. Why not?'" Money kicked back his stingy-brimmed hat with a nervy hand. "By then, Ragland had 'em all convinced I wasn't nothing but a first-class thug, anyhow; all just to cover his tracks."

"But Daddy and the church got you out early that first time—"

"Sure they did—to save face." Money protested. "But if Deacon Ragland had had his way, I'd still be locked up."

"Maybe," Melissa said sternly, "but whatever the reason, Money, you've got two strikes, now—"

"I know, Missy! I know!" Money blared. "No third strike!"

CHAPTER 17
Gold Nugget

"Whoa! It sure is hot out there, Pastor." Wanza barreled into Pastor Meadow's study swinging a fan from side-to-side in one hand and holding a can of soda in the other. "I was hoping the spring rains would come and cool us off this year, but it doesn't look likely." She helped herself to a tissue from the blue box on his crowded desk and used it as a coaster to wedge her soda can into the mess. "I sure do thank your wife for putting me on your schedule early today. We need to talk."

"You alright, Sister Wanza?" The pastor's thick brows crossed. As usual, Wanza was taking up more air in the room than he was prepared to deal with, and he'd been patiently awaiting his turn to speak. "You seem a little flustered this morning."

"I am flustered." Wanza spread her pounds into the guest chair across from his desk. Her yellow tent dress was barely able to cover her knees, and the blonde-tint wig she'd worn for the occasion was making it difficult for her to see out of one eye. "It's that Y, I tell you," she said, fiddling with her bangs. "She's over there at that Center acting like them kids don't belong to her. She's acting like they're her brother and sister, or something. She wants to stay foot-loose-and-fancy-free while everybody else does all the work. But those are *her* kids! And they're *her* responsibility!"

"So you're still volunteering at the Center, huh?"

"Like I told you, Pastor," Wanza said defensively, "Mrs. Lawson—she's the director over there, you know—she didn't even assign me to Y's case. She's got me working in the front office on them books; and let me tell you, they really need help." She took a long swig of her soda. "But you best believe I keep my ears to the ground, and I hear how those case workers be talking 'bout them girls; 'specially, the ones that ain't cutting it. And Y is leading the pack."

"Oh?"

"Yeah, Pastor. Y is turning out to be a straight-up user." Wanza blustered. "They say as long as she can get her hair done; her nails did; and swindle somebody outta free child care, she's a happy camper. But you'd better not ask her to do one, blessed thing 'cause it ain't gonna happen."

"Is that right?" The pastor said coolly.

"That's right." Wanza fumed. "Y's taking everything them folk have to offer—free food, free room and board, free clothes, free child care—but she won't give nothing back. She won't wash the dishes; she won't help in the nursery; she won't go to school, or look for a job. She doesn't even want to make up her own bed!"

"So that's the rap on Y, huh?"

"Sure is." Wanza steamed. "And she was doing the same stuff at my house, but I cut her some slack 'cause she was so big with that baby. But she's had the baby, now, and she still won't do a thing over at that Center to let those folk know she appreciates all they're doing for her and her kids. They say she spends her time figuring out tricks and lies to keep the benefits coming—she's sick; the baby's sick; she'll start next week; the computer's down—anything except get up off her rear." Wanza huffed. "It's embarrassing, Pastor, 'specially after all you did to get her into that place. You've gotta talk some sense into her 'cause I'm sick o' trying. And I know all those people over there at that Center are sick o' fooling with her trifling—"

"So what do you think I should do, Wanza?" Pastor Meadows pulled her up short.

"I don't know." Wanza sucked on her soda. "But if she doesn't shape up, they're gonna kick her straight up outta there. Then what?" She plopped down her can. "They've been trying to fix it so they can set her up in her own apartment, but they can't do that 'til she shows some signs of being able to take care of herself and them kids."

"So that's Y's situation." Pastor Meadows folded his arms across his wide chest. "What's yours?"

"Huh?" Wanza's eyes flashed at him from behind her troublesome bangs. "Whatcha mean?"

"That's why I called you in here today, Wanza." Pastor Meadows explained. "Not to talk about Y, but to talk about you."

"Well, I'm making it." Wanza quieted. "Me and the boys...we doing alright."

"Is *alright* enough for you, Wanza?"

"I don't understand what you mean," she said, letting her guard slip a bit.

"I've watched how you take great care of your boys." Pastor Meadows smiled. "And I've watched how you've worried over Y—"

"Well, somebody needs to." Wanza refueled her argument. "Because Y doesn't seem to know how to take care of herself and them kids—"

"I grant you, Y's in a difficult situation right now." Pastor Meadows agreed. "She doesn't seem to know how to make the best of a good thing. But is Y's situation your responsibility?"

"Huh?"

"I know you were moved to action to help Y based on my sermons on The Good Samaritan."

"Right." Wanza nodded.

"So I feel it's my responsibility to be sure you understand the full story." Pastor Meadows reared his thick frame back into his squishy leather chair.

"Whatcha mean?" Wanza gaped, slack-jawed.

"Where The Good Samaritan's job started...and where it stopped."

"Huh?"

"Look at the story with me, again, Wanza, step by step."

"O-kay."

"The Good Samaritan saw the injured man's needs and responded."

"Right."

"He had compassion and took immediate steps to improve the injured man's situation, like you did for Y."

"Right." Wanza nodded.

"But look at what The Good Samaritan didn't do." The pastor ticked off his points on the stubby fingers of his right hand. "One...he didn't stick around wringing his hands over the injured man. Two...he went his own way, handling his own affairs while making provision to leave the injured man in good hands. Three...he didn't make a special trip back to see about the injured man, or keep tabs on him after the fact." Pastor Meadows laced his fingers together and set them under his chin for leverage. "Are you with me so far?"

"Yes." Wanza nodded dubiously.

"So you see, Wanza, our compassion for others does not equal worry or constant care over their situation. It's a commitment to do our best to help them get out of immediate danger, like you did for Y." Pastor Meadows held Wanza's eyes in his. "And then we must let go and entrust their lives to God, just as we entrust our own lives to Him. God loves Y just like God loves you."

"So you're saying I'm doing too much to help Y?"

"No, I'm saying you've done all you can to help Y." Pastor Meadows reasoned patiently. "We can help her, but we can't heal her. Whatever is broken in Y, only the Lord can fix. Her issues are way too deep for any of us to touch. And, sometimes, we can do more harm than good by getting in the way of the lesson the Lord is teaching. Besides, you running around trying to play God for Y can only hinder her growth—"

"But—"

"You can't save Y any more than I could save you, Wanza." Pastor Meadows reminded her. "When you came in my office as mad as a hornet at the injustice you felt Douglas had done you, I couldn't help you. All I could do was point you to Jesus—"

"Yes, but—"

"Because each of us has to put our own, personal faith in the Lord." Pastor Meadow's patience was wearing thin. "I can't do it for you, and you can't do it for me."

"I know that—"

"So then don't you think it's time to entrust Y and her children into God's hands?" Pastor Meadows drilled. "We can't make Y believe, or feel, or do what we think—"

"But she doesn't know what's good for her—"

"Wanza!" Pastor Meadows blared; counting it a blessing he no longer had hair, because this well-meaning woman would certainly make him snatch it all out by the roots. "We don't know what's good for Y. We don't know what *good* is!"

"Is everything alright in here?" Candi Meadows stuck her head in the door to check out the ruckus. She smiled and closed it, again, when her husband waved her off.

"Can't you see, Wanza." Beads of sweat were starting to pop out on Pastor Meadows' round head. "You're trying to keep the ball from rolling off the table because you think that's a *good* thing—"

"But it is a good thing—"

"But sometimes the ball needs to roll off the table for the *best* thing to happen—"

"Huh?"

"None of His friends thought it was a good thing for Him, either, but where would we be if Jesus hadn't been crucified...for us?"

"Oh-h!" Wanza's mouth rounded in astonishment.

"Only God knows what's best, Wanza!!" Pastor Meadows snatched a tissue from his blue box, mopped his sweaty brow and reeled in his straining emotions. "Only God knows what's best."

When Wanza's eyes finally flushed with understanding, her shoulders sagged. "So I'm s'pose to just stand by and watch while she ruins her life...gets herself and them kids kicked outta that Center?"

"From what you told me, you've talked to Y about this." Pastor Meadows' voice drew into an even line. "Now, it's time to talk to the Lord about it and trust Him to work it out for Y, for her kids...and for you."

"Me?" Wanza bristled.

"Yes, you, Wanza." Pastor Meadows leveled. "You can't put your life on hold by hanging out in Y's troubles—"

"But I've been trying to do the right thing—"

"You've been busying yourself, true; so you don't have to deal with your own situation," Pastor Meadows said bluntly. "But that's not the way, Wanza. You've got lots to consider for yourself—college, career, profession, ministry, travel, relationships, whatever. You have a life to live...and not in the shadow of anybody else's."

"But how am I s'pose to know what to do?"

"The Lord has a plan for each of us, but we have to deal with the sins that can short-circuit our blessings." Pastor Meadows enumerated. "Bitterness, hatred, envy—"

"Or being so mad and sad you wanna check-out 'cause you can't have things your way—"

"What?" Pastor Meadows stopped cold. "You'd never hurt yourself—"

"Me? No way!" The blonde fringe on Wanza's wig shook vigorously. "I might pluck your eyes out and feed 'em to the pigeons, but I ain't never gonna hurt me...not ever."

"That's good news." Pastor Meadows relaxed and picked up where he'd left off. "And when we pray through the sins that try to block our blessings—turn those rascals over to the Lord—then His plan for our lives will become clearer and clearer."

"It will?" Wanza said timidly.

"Yes, Wanza." The pastor smiled, glad to finally be getting through to her. "I know you're used to a tit-for-tat world where people only love you for what you can do for them. But Jesus doesn't operate like that. He came to give us love, and He's got all the love we'll ever need."

"But—" The words croaked in Wanza's throat. "I'm afraid—"

"I know." Pastor Meadows stood and took both of Wanza's hands into his own. "Learning to consider your own needs when you've spent a lifetime trying to earn the love of others, it's a change that doesn't come easy." He squeezed her hands tightly. "So let's pray about it...okay...together."

CHAPTER 18

Gold Star

A few months later, Douglas' eyes were glued on Wanza when the ushers opened the floodgates and she came bustling down the aisle at True Vine with all the other late comers. She was traveling solo because she'd already dropped the boys off at Children's Church, which had caused her to run late for the Call to Worship. And by the time the stragglers were admitted, the senior choir, accompanied by the melodious strands of the full orchestra, was already in high gear, belting out the hymn of preparation for the morning, "Come Ye Disconsolate…earth has no sorrow that heaven cannot heal."

Wanza was wearing a sleeveless, color-blocked skimmer, which zipped from the hem to her full, flush cleavage. It silhouetted her slimming waistline, wide hips and thick calves in her designer platform wedgies. And since her standout features were starting to trim down—the way Douglas always liked them—his eyes had her on lockdown. *Oh, how I remember my nights with you, Miss Wanza!* But when Melissa trailed his line of sight to Wanza, she tugged on Douglas' elbow to regain his undivided attention.

Despite the usher's assistance, Wanza was having a little trouble navigating to an empty seat because the bangs on her long brunette wig kept flopping down into her eyes. "Psst." Willamina Redd reached out and touched her on the elbow. She scooted over and made room for Wanza on the end of her pew.

"Oh, thank you, so much," Wanza mumbled as she rummaged around to find a suitable spot on the tightly-packed row for her new Gucci purse, which matched her shoes.

"My pleasure." Miss Redd smiled.

When Douglas' eyes fished around for another sighting of the new-and-improved Wanza, they fell upon Miss Redd instead. Her long, red hair was free-flowing like a tigress' mane, and the glow on her gorgeous, porcelain face reminded him of the radiance of sunbeams. In that instant, he was spellbound...again.

Wanza gave a quiet chuckle when she noticed Melissa snatching on Douglas' arm to turn his roving eyes back in her direction, and it brought back a sharp reminder of Sundays past. "Listen, Miss Redd," Wanza whispered, "I've been meaning to tell you how sorry I am for causing such a scene that day you joined True Vine. It was shameful of me—"

"Call me, Willamina," she whispered. "And, don't you go worrying your pretty, little head over that none." She assured her. "It's Wanza, right?"

"Yes." Wanza nodded, surprised a superstar would remember her name.

"Well, Wanza, I play some of the toughest honky-tonks in Texas," Willamina buzzed in a low whisper. "And when those cowboys and goat-ropers get to going, I know how tempers can flare."

"Ooo-wee," Wanza whispered, "I sure would love to see the insides of one of them honky-tonks, just once."

"Well, I play 'em all." Willamina hummed. "In fact, my schedule's so tight right, now, I've got to talk to Pastor about what I can do to help out at the church, since my time is so limited."

"I'm sure he'll come up with something." Wanza eked out a giggle, keenly aware of Pastor Meadow's intense drive. "He sure is helping me get some things sorted out right now. He even has me going back to college."

"Well, good for you!" Willamina smiled and drew out a business card from her leather satchel. She handed it to Wanza. "Tell you what. I'm gonna be at Billy Bob's in Fort Worth next month—

Fourth of July weekend. And if you wanna come and be my guest, just give me a call."

"You'd do that for me?" Wanza said in an excited whisper.

"Sure thing, Girl." Willamina nudged her playfully in the ribs. "Then I'll be sure to have at least one friend in the audience." She tittered. "And after the set, you can hang out with us at the W Hotel. We'll let our hair down; have some fun. How does that sound to ya?"

"Fun?" Wanza repeated dreamily. "I sure could use some o' that."

"Then give me a call." Willamina buzzed. "And if my agent, Boo-Ray, happens to answer, you just give him your name, and he'll make all the arrangements for ya."

"Wow, I sure will!" Wanza whispered.

"Shh!" An older lady with a brand new aqua hat and suit to match rolled up on them from the rear of their pew. "Pay attention!" She sizzled. "Pastor is speaking!"

Willamina and Wanza squeezed hands in solidarity, like sisters. And then, obediently, they turned their eyes to the pulpit.

CHAPTER 19
Gold Brick

"If you came over here to fuss at me, again, Miss Wanza, I ain't trying to hear it." Y turned her back as soon as her door creaked opened at the Center. She resituated her slender form on her assigned, twin-sized dormitory bed. The white sheets looked as though they hadn't been changed in weeks.

"Where's Austin?" Wanza said as she bustled in.

"Day care. Where else?"

"And little Teesha?"

"She hangin' out with my buddy at the end o' the hall. She got a baby, too, you know."

"Have you signed up for school, or put out any work applications?"

"Yeah, I'm working on it." Y shifted further away from Wanza and her interminable questions.

"So what're you doing today?" Wanza needled.

"Chillin'."

"But don't you see, Y." Wanza flung up her hands. "Sitting around and surviving on these people's handouts is taking away your power to be all you can be for yourself and your kids—"

"Oh, here we go, again—"

"But, Y, you know how hard it was for Pastor Meadows to get you into this place—"

"Ugh!" Y pushed her face deeper into her pillow.

"And, Y, you need to start bonding…connecting with your kids. You need to get to know them and let them get to know you—read to them; talk to them; listen to them; spend time with them—because to a child, time equals love. You need to be a parent!"

"And I'm just so sure you can tell me all I need to know 'bout making a family, huh, Miss Wanza?" Y said, dripping sarcasm like hot wax onto Wanza's failed marriage.

"But, Y," Wanza pleaded more earnestly, "don't you understand? These folk will kick you out—"

"Enough, Miss Wanza! Dag!" Y covered her ears with her well-manicured hands. "I got this, okay? I told you. I got these case workers eating outta my hand."

The hair rose on the back of Wanza's neck. She wanted to grab Y and shake some sense into her, but instead she breathed deeply and refocused. "Well, anyway," Wanza finally said, "that's not why I stopped by."

"Good!" Y jeered.

"I came by to tell you my news." Wanza's voice spiked with excitement.

"Your news?" Y turned over to face her because this she wanted to hear.

"I've been praying with Pastor Meadows and his wife, Candi, you know." Wanza pulled up a chair close to her bedside. "Trying to figure out what the Lord has for me—not for my children, or my past—but for me, here and now."

"That so?" Y smirked.

"And I don't know exactly what it is, but I've cut back volunteering here at the Center from three days to one."

"O-kay." Y tooted her lips and twirled her neck in disinterest.

"And I've enrolled at TSU, again," Wanza said excitedly. "I didn't realize it, but I only need 60 college credits to complete my degree. I can be finished by March 2016—less than a year away."

"That so?" Y sniffed.

"I've got all the credits I need for my minor in Business, but I've changed my major to Sociology and Family Development!"

"Oh, really!" Y was starting to get swept up in Wanza's enthusiasm.

"And I'm enjoying my classes so much—being around the other students, being able to exchange ideas, share my experiences—"

"Well, you sure do sound different, Miss Wanza." Y granted.

"Well—" Wanza gave her a cheeky grin. "If I want to be heard by *them*, I have to put my Ebonics on the back burner, at least for now, and take up English as a second language." She teased. "But make no mistake, Miss Y, I can swang it either way, Gurrlfriend."

"I just bet you can, Miss Wanza." Y snickered.

"And I've been learning so much from Pastor Meadows and his wife," Wanza said more seriously. "You know how mad I was about Doug and all that—"

"Do I?" Y snorted. "You still waiting for Miss Melissa to apologize to you?"

"Nope." Wanza flattened. "I figure I won't live that long, so I've forgiven her completely, without it."

"Oh?" Y's eyes widened.

"Pastor Meadows helped me see that, too." Wanza shrugged. "Everybody in our trial is heaven sent. We can't hate the players. We can only love the Saviour, who shows up strong on our behalf...in spite of what they did. Learn the lesson. Move on. Until the next time...because there will be a next time." Wanza nodded. "And if we don't get bitter, every round will grow us bigger and better—"

"I don't know 'bout all that." Y sighed, signaling the return of her boredom. "But I see you done gone natural. I ain't never seen you without one of yo' fancy wigs."

"You like it?" Wanza glimmered. "I'm not hiding behind all that fake hair, anymore."

"Um-hmm." Y considered her new look. "You got a real pretty face; nice cheeks; and your short hair frames it real good. You use a perm?"

"Nope. No chemicals for me." Wanza patted her soft, little 'fro. "I thought it was about time for me to get back to my roots; get in touch with the real me."

"That's good—"

"And Pastor Meadows taught me something else, too," Wanza said excitedly.

"What's that?"

"How to quit running around in circles…stressing over everything…fussing over you." Wanza winked. "So I spend my time, now, asking the Lord to handle stuff." Wanza stood up and shimmied the slimmer version of her shapely hips. "Bam!

"Hmm…looks like you been hittin' the gym, too, Miss Wanza." Y giggled. "Looking good, Gurrl! And that outfit you're rockin' is on fleek—"

"Say what?" Wanza stopped, mid-turn.

"Translation for dummies," Y muttered under her breath. "Your outfit, Miss Wanza, it's fly…you sharp…you looking good—"

"Oh, I get it." Wanza lifted up her chin. "But do you really think so?"

"Yeah." Y grinned. "You blazin' hot!

"Well, I've been catching on to how the other students dress." Wanza completed her full turn in the cute flare top, skinny jeans and platform sandals she was wearing. "And I've lost 30 pounds," she said proudly. "Eating healthy…cutting out all those donuts and sodas—"

"Oh, so that's why you ain't as hyper as you used to be?" Y viewed her mentor with new eyes. "You off them sugar highs—"

"Don't know." Wanza flashed Y a sweet smile. "Guess so."

"Mr. Douglas seen you looking so good?"

"Who knows?" Wanza shrugged. "But maybe, I was using my fat to get back at him…eating to hide my pain." She smirked. "Or maybe, I just didn't want to be attractive to him anymore…destroy the one thing he always liked about me…using my body like a weapon. But no matter, I'm done destroying me—"

"So…now—" Y giggled with a wicked twinkle in her eye. "Whatcha gonna do when all these *new* men start rolling up on you?"

"Well, if he's 20, I'll say, 'Hey, Boy…where yo' mama?" Wanza bounced back into her Ebonics. Her dormant sense of humor was also making a comeback. "And if he's 30, I'll say, 'Hey, Boy…where yo' daddy?" She winked. "And if he's 40, I'll say, "Hey, Boy…what yo' name is?"

"Hee-hee-hee!" Y doubled over in a fit of laughter. "Miss Wanza, you are one, hot mess!" She cried, wiping her eyes on her motley bed sheet. "But if it takes school and a new man to get you off my case, well, I'm all for it!"

CHAPTER 20
Solid Gold

"Melissa! Melissa! Wake up!" Douglas shouted as he turned on every light from the downstairs foyer to their elegant upstairs bedroom suite.

"What?" Melissa popped up in their plush bed. "What is it, Douglas? What's wrong?"

Douglas bounced down on the bed beside her, ignoring her warnings about spoiling the embroidered satin coverlet. "There's nothing wrong, Melissa! Everything's right. Just right!" His raucous laughter bounced off their cavernous bedroom walls, filling up the emptiness that lived there.

Melissa brushed back her flowing hair and sat up straight against her pillows. She was laughing, now, too; although, she didn't know why. She loved it when Douglas got like this. He was drunk with success—so wild, so passionate, so sexy. "What? What is it, Babe," she begged. "Tell me! Tell me!"

"The meeting couldn't have gone better!" Douglas started.

"With Willamina Redd and Willie Nealy?"

"Yes!" Douglas' voice rolled thick and heavy like dark molasses. "For a long time I've been talking to Fisk University about having a concert-to-beat-all-concerts to celebrate their 150th Anniversary—next year in 2016."

"Where'd you get the idea?"

"I gained a lot of respect for the Fisk students who had dual enrollment during my years at Vandy." Douglas rubbed his hands together excitedly. "And besides, any institution of higher learning that manages to survive, thrive and turn-out such brilliant minds for 150 years—HBCU or not—deserves to be celebrated!"

"Here-Here!" Melissa mirrored her husband's enthusiasm. "And their Sesquicentennial Celebration will be next year?"

"Yes! May of next year to be exact—just less than a year from now." Douglas' words were spinning like flaming rockets. "But it's got to be the bomb! To be effective and raise the kind of money that Fisk needs for scholarships and operations, this concert's got to literally set the music industry on its ear. It's got to be the kind of joint that nobody in this world will want to miss. Absolutely nobody!"

"Okay!"

"And I want it to showcase the full array of talent that Star Music Promotions International has to offer. I want it to be everything from acapella Negro Spirituals by the world-renowned Fisk Jubilee Singers; to R&B and Blues; to modern-day Rap and Hip-Hop; and to the pride of Nashville—Country."

"So you're planning to have it right here in Nashville?"

"Of course!" Douglas raved. "This concert will truly solidify Nashville's fame as Music City USA, not to mention what it'll do for Star Music Promotions in this city...in this nation...in this world!"

"So what's gotten you so excited?"

"Well, to pull something off like this, you need a zinger of a closer." Douglas rolled. "You need a crescendo...a closing number that pops! You need...*Dah-Dah!*"

"And you've got it?"

"Boy-Howdy!" Douglas hopped up off the bed and paced the floor, too excited to sit any longer. "Tonight, Willie Nealy accepted Willamina Redd's request for him to perform a duet with her as the closing number of my concert—"

"*Dah-Dah!*"

"And Willie Nealy will help us get permission to have my concert-of-the-century on the Grand Ole Opry's biggest stage!"

Douglas expounded, finding it hard to catch his breath. "I think I'll make it black tie, and the tickets will go for $250 a pop. It'll go primetime, pay per view…you name it! The spotlight will be on Fisk University; Music City USA; and my talent stable will get worldwide publicity, sending Star Music Promotions International soaring to the moon and back. This will truly be a *Grand* production!"

"The concert's going to broadcast all over the world?" Melissa hitched her wagon onto his fervor. "Wow! You'll be the envy of the whole music industry!"

"You've got that right! We'll set a new gold standard for live performances. This concert will be talked about and envied for years to come!" Douglas' eyes caught fire. "And it's all because of Willamina Redd."

The mere mention of her name set Douglas to boiling all over, again. Being around her—smelling her rich perfume, getting lost in those crystal blue eyes—it was all he could do to keep his hands to himself. He knew he couldn't be straight with her about his intentions. He'd have to ease up on her, like a tiger on its prey. But the woman was in his head, in his dreams, in his every desire; and, now, she was crawling her way into his heart.

Unlike Melissa and Wanza, Douglas felt Willamina was his equal in every way—drive, passion, understanding. And her connections in the music business—his business—were impeccable. And it didn't hurt that she was gorgeous and classy beyond his wildest dreams. *I've been dropping hints for months. I thought tonight would be the night…we had such a great time together…so much in common…so much to share. But she knows I'm married, and she won't let me get close. She won't let me get close enough to lock-up her mind, but—*

"Doug-las." Melissa crooned, interrupting his sweet reverie. "Come on over here." She rubbed the top of her satin coverlet, not realizing his body was present on Legend's Way, but his mind was three streets over on Peacock Place. "Come on over here and give me all your loving." She cooed.

Douglas was on fire for Miss Redd, but he realized his wife would have to serve as the next best thing. So he took out his frustrations on Melissa—all night long.

CHAPTER 21

Golden Tears

"Missy, I been doin' some thinkin'." Money slurred his words over his cheap tracfone. He'd ditched work for the day and was camped out on the tiny cot in his pea-sized room at the unsavory Legion Arms Hotel on the rough side of downtown Nashville. He hated the place. But, today, it had become his sanctuary from the nagging thoughts that haunted him.

"Sounds to me like you've been doing some drinking." Melissa's tense words reverberated over the bluetooth in her Lexus.

"Well...I might o' had a li'l rum toddy...or two...or three." Money snickered. "But who's counting?"

"I'm hanging up, now, Money." Melissa's voice oozed with irritation. "It's not enough that Douglas is all caught up with his *mega-concert-of-the-century*. I've also had the day from hell with his hood-rat clientele, and I barely have the energy to drive myself home to an empty house. And then here you come, Money, slurping and slurring—"

"But who else can I talk to, Missy?" Money's voice pleaded. "Don't I take time to listen...when you wanna talk?"

"Oh, all right." Melissa snapped. "I'll give you until I pull into my garage—"

"You see." Money babbled like a child. "I know why I got my second strike—"

"I know, too," Melissa said flatly. "Because you were caught selling drugs—"

"Wasn't sellin'." Money sniffed. "Just holdin'."

"Uh-huh." Melissa jeered. "Nobody believes that but you, Money."

"I know. I know. Nobody believes me." Money's voice ran the scale from whining to sniveling. "But it's the God's-honest truth, Missy. I swear."

"But it got you three more years behind bars...and your second strike."

"When I got out the first time...remember?" Money rubbed his nose, and his voice clouded over. "That was right before the new Prez stopped by our church after his speech at the University of Tennessee—"

"Oh, yes. I'll never forget that." Melissa's voice brightened. "It was 2009; the first year of President Obama's first term." She recalled. "We were all so elated. I came down for a visit from Nashville. You were fresh out of jail. And our church was the talk of the whole country."

"Don't even know why the POTUS came to Tennessee." Money muttered. "Other than the fact he was black...and new...and trying to prove he was gonna be fair to the southern states, even the ones that didn't vote him in—"

"President Obama was so handsome; his wife, Michelle, so sheik; and their little girls, oh, so precious." Melissa gushed. "And their visit to Faith Freewill gave Daddy a lock as the premier black pastor in Knoxville. And I thought Mother would just faint dead away from all the publicity, the television cameras...and the newspaper photos featuring her standing right next to the first black President of the United States of America!"

"Yeah, and I think that's when it all started to break bad—"

"Huh?"

"You were working in Nashville, Missy, so you don't know the whole story." Money sighed. "But I was there; fresh out o' jail and back living in that whacked-out house with Mother and Daddy—"

"But you didn't have anywhere else to go—"

"Did you know Deacon Ragland was stealing from the church?" Money skidded into an abrupt about-face.

"What?" Melissa stomped on her brakes and nearly got rear-ended.

"Yep." Money recalled. "After President Obama came, the church membership shot-up and so did the offering baskets. And I guess it was just too much temptation for Deacon Ragland and his two cronies. They were in charge of counting the money after service, you know. And one Sunday, Daddy walked in on 'em; caught 'em sticking cash in their pockets. They had it divvied up three ways."

"How do you know this?" Melissa challenged.

"Overheard Daddy telling Mother…when I was hiding behind our secret door…smoking—"

"So why didn't Daddy tell the church?" Melissa quizzed.

"He told Mother that Deacon Ragland threatened to tell the church a pack o' lies on him if he let anybody know what they were doing—"

"What kind of lies?"

"Well, Daddy couldn't tell Mother." Money reminded her. "But Deacon Ragland had the low-down on Daddy and his mistress; remember?"

"Oh, that's right." Melissa strained to keep her focus; aware that Money's stories often took a decidedly circuitous route, especially when he'd been in his cup. "So what did Daddy do?"

"I guess he put up with it as long as his conscience could stand it." Money surmised. "But it wasn't long before he got in Deacon Ragland's face and told him if he didn't stop skimming off the top, he'd have to put the church on notice." Money let out a low whistle. "And then, Missy, everything turned bottom-upwards—"

"What happened?" Melissa flapped. "And why didn't you tell me?"

"You were in Nashville...and believe me...you didn't really wanna know." Money slowed. "But hold onto your wig, Missy, 'cause this here's gonna be a bumpy ride." His voice hollowed, and Money recounted his story as if it were the tail-end of a nightmare.

****

"It was a bright and sunny first Sunday in May the day the whole world changed as we knew it." Money recalled. "Seems like over a thousand members had turned out at Faith Freewill to take communion. Everybody was pumped. Daddy was sweating and sputtering up in the pulpit something like, 'If you confess your sins, the Lord is faithful and just to forgive you your sins and cleanse you from all unrighteousness!'"

"Well, that passed." Money chomped on his toothpick. "The offering was lifted. And everybody was starting to quieten down to take communion. And then Daddy stood back up at the pulpit. I thought Mother would raise up outta her seat, but she managed to keep her place."

"I'll never forget it," Money said, as though he were in a trance. "Mother had on a white dress and a big flowered black and white polka-dot hat. Sister Pearly Sistrunk, sitting in her usual spot right behind Mother, had a big orange concoction on her head, with some kind o' frilly yellow dress...looking like a big ole banana."

"But, anyhoo." Money snorted. "Daddy stands back up and says, 'Church, I have some unfortunate news to report. I hate to do it on Communion Sunday; but, nevertheless, it needs to be said to clear my conscience before we receive the emblems.'"

"Next thing you know, Sister Sistrunk raises her hand and stands up," Money said, mocking her pretentious delivery. "She sniffed back some fake tears and said, 'If this is a Sunday for clearing our consciences, then I also have something I need to confess.'"

"And with that, the whole church dropped open like one big mouth. Nobody was used to hearing true confessions, not in the sanctuary, of all places. Sister Sistrunk said, 'I have been having a sorted and shameful affair. I'm not proud of it. In fact, I'm pretty convicted. And I cannot take communion with it on my heart.'"

"She blew her nose into her lace hankie, caught her breath and kept going. 'But since Deacon Ragland and I have become engaged to be married.' She flashed some itty-bitty ring sitting on her left hand, and Daddy fell back into his big chair before he could hit the floor. 'I think it only fair that I confess that I've been having this shameful and sorted affair with none other than...Pastor Walter Mann.'"

"Well, the whole church fell out." Money recounted. "There was whooping and hollering, fainting and cussing, like you ain't never seen before in your life. And women were fanning Mother trying to keep her upright. Needless to say, communion was called off for lack of interest."

"And when we finally got home, I knew there was gonna be one, big blow-out." Money mumbled. "So I hid behind our secret door, 'cause I knew Mother would be saying words to that man that would make me wanna knock her out." Money's voice grated. "And I'm cleaning this up to tell it to you, Missy, 'cause our mother low-rated that po' man with words I don't even let cross my lips."

"She came at him like a she-cat, clawin' and slashin'." Money's voice swelled. "'Walter Mann, you are one stupid so-and-so! How in the world could you allow yourself to be backed into a corner like this? Before you even tried to confront Deacon Ragland at the church, you should've had all your facts straight...all your ducks in a row. You know what kind o' worm that man is.' Mother screeched like a banshee. 'Didn't you know he was crawling into Pearly Sistrunk's bed right behind you every week? You did your creeping on Tuesday nights, and he did his on Fridays.'"

"By this time, Mother was screaming so loud the walls were rocking, and Daddy was as quiet as a mouse. 'Yes, I knew, you big dummy!' She yelled. 'But I didn't say a word. Why should I? It wasn't no skin off my nose if you wanted to act the fool, just as long as it didn't hurt me or my church. But that's why I kept telling you not to call Ragland out. I told you to leave that weasel alone! Those few dollars that him and those other two thieves were pocketing weren't worth you destroying your whole career. But nooo, you have to go and try to have a conscience about him stealing. Why didn't you have a conscience about your whoring around?'"

"Mother was on a roll, now, and she flung it all up in Daddy's face. 'And you can bet Ragland put Pearly Mae up to this by telling her that lie that he's gonna marry her. He wouldn't marry that slut if she was golden. His wife's been dead five years, and he hasn't married anybody up 'til now. He's having too much fun diddling with every woman at the church—married and single. And if he ever were to marry, you can best believe it won't be to Pearly Mae Sistrunk!'"

"And then, just like that, Mother zigzagged and started building their cover story. 'But be that as it may, Walter Mann,' she said, 'you can still fight that dog, Ragland. I've been keeping a close watch on him. And with what I know about him, the Deacons and Trustees wouldn't dare try to put you out. If you play your cards right, you can retain your position as Senior Pastor of Faith Freewill. I'll stand by your side so you can keep your job. I don't care what that tramp, Pearly Sistrunk, has to say. You can put all those jackals to shame and put yourself back on top. Church folk are stupid! Church folk forget!'"

"Daddy didn't say a mumbling word to her or anyone else after that." Money's voice sounded ghostly. "He was stricken in a way I'd never seen before. Maybe, he really did love Pearly Sistrunk; or maybe, he felt trapped by the things he didn't wanna do; or maybe, his own lies got him backed into a corner; or maybe with everything he'd put up with over the years from Mother, this was the last and final straw. I don't know. But from that day forward, our Daddy was a broken man." Money's toothpick flattened. "The church was in such an uproar, the Trustees had a meeting to call for his resignation. Mother wouldn't hear of it, of course, so she told him, 'We'll fight this thing, tooth and nail, Walter Mann! We'll fight this, and we will win!'"

"But two Sundays later, Daddy was dead." Money coughed. "His death was ruled accidental, due to an allergic reaction. You know, Daddy was deathly allergic to peanuts. And Daddy knew it, too. So why did I find him sprawled out on the kitchen floor with a jar of peanut butter in one hand and a spoon in the other?" Money hiccupped back his tears. "Mother was out shopping. Don't know how long he'd been in that condition. The coroner said they couldn't determine how it happened. His epi-pen was in his pocket. But, you see, it was me who dumped the jar and spoon in the corner dumpster before the ambulance got there…trying to spare Mother the embarrassment."

Money coughed, again, attempting to regain his balance. "At the funeral, when you and Mother were nosing up to all the dignitaries, Mother Whatnot cornered me, again—cheap perfume and all. Pee-uw!" He snorted. "She seemed to sense something was up. So she pinned me with her li'l beady eyes and said, 'Son, don't let none o' this turn you 'round. You can be born at the church-house; sleep on the altar; bathe in the baptismal pool; and eat off the communion plates. But all o' that don't make you no child o' God. When this day comes—and it surely will for us all—you got to know Jesus for yo'self.'"

****

"Five days later, I get popped for possession of felony-weight heroine…with intent to distribute." Money fought his way back to the present; the weight of his memories nearly dragging him under. "But the drugs were for me, Missy—for my own personal use." He confided. "I wasn't trying to sell nothing. I swear. Maybe, I was trying to take myself out, too. I don't know." Money breathed, long and hard. "But anyhoo…it got me my strike number two."

Melissa had been sitting in her closed garage for over ten minutes, tears streaming, listening to Money fill in the blanks on the sordid history of her perfect family; and she was mourning his tortured soul, which had borne the weight of it for such a long time—alone. When he was done, she almost wished she'd kept the engine running.

CHAPTER 22

Golden Dagger

"Oh, Lord, I've got to change my doctor!" Wanza shook her head as she strolled back into the trendy waiting room of The Barrows Clinic. "They just let anybody in here."

"Oh, no!" Melissa said under her breath.

"Hey 'Lissa." Wanza sauntered over to where she was sitting. "What you in for?"

"Keep stepping, Wanza." Melissa swirled the pages in her magazine. "I'm not interested in having a cat fight with you in the middle of my doctor's office."

"No worries." Wanza shrugged. "I'm not mad at you anymore. But come on now, you know I've got to razz you every now and then." She let her voice drop. "You did steal my husband."

"Same song. Different verse." Melissa shifted away from her and re-crossed her elegant legs under her skimpy mini.

"But you don't have to worry about ole Wanza, anymore." She chuckled. "I've got bigger fish to fry, now. And I really do forgive you, Girl." She stood back in her shapely, thick calves. "In fact, losing Doug might've been the best thing that ever happened to me—"

"Then why're you still eyeballing us at church?" Melissa squawked.

"I'm looking at you," Wanza whispered sweetly, "because you're getting so thin, and your hair is looking so…picky. Are you okay?"

"And I see you've lost a few *needed* pounds yourself." Melissa deflected. "And you've rid yourself of those very unattractive wigs—"

"Fifty pounds gone, to be exact," Wanza said proudly. "And I'm so glad you approve of my new 'do." She patted her fluffy 'fro and shifted her curves to set her trim waistline and shapely butt on full display in her new red sundress. "Been trying to eat right so I don't have to take all these pills they try to force down our throats. And I'm getting a little exercise, too, so I can keep up with those busy boys of mine." Wanza grinned. "You getting any exercise?"

"No." Melissa raised her beautiful brows. "Too busy working with my husband—"

"Well, you'd better take good care of yourself." Wanza's eyes fell on Melissa's platinum-set, five-carat wedding band. "Because I know from experience," she whispered, "just because you've got a husband...doesn't mean you've got a friend—"

"What-ever!" Melissa sparked.

"I'm in for my annual." Wanza repeated. "What're you in for?"

"I don't think that's any of your business." Melissa sniped. "But if you must know...and if it will make you walk away...I'm here for my well-woman's exam, just like you." She lied. She'd been seeing Dr. Barrows every two weeks to get some very painful and expensive fertility shots. The doctor had determined it was their best course of action since Douglas wouldn't consent to any tests.

"Um-hmm." Wanza shifted and gave Melissa a long look of concern. "Well, I know at least one thing you're not in here for." She pursed her thick lips. "You are *not* pregnant."

"And just how do you know that?" Melissa's neck bobbled violently. "You don't have a clue—"

"I may not have a clue about a lot of things." Wanza's eyes flashed. "But this one thing I do know. You will *not* be having any babies with Douglas Grand."

"Hmph!" Melissa swirled her shiny finger to the exist. "Wanza, just pay your bill and go—"

"Because D-o-u-g." Wanza tossed his name like it was a vile thing. "He had a vasectomy after Donovan was born. He said he didn't want any more babies—"

"Kids! Kids!" Melissa was trembling with humiliation. "That's all you baby-mamas ever think about. I'm not into babies. I'm a career woman!"

"Well, okay, *Ms. Career-Woman*." Wanza turned away with a flourish. "This here baby-mama is about to pay her bill and go home to her babies." She shot Melissa a satisfied glance over her shoulder on her way out. "What're you going home to do?"

Melissa would've fainted dead away, right then and there, if nobody had been looking. She stiffened her back and swallowed down the bile that was burning in her belly. When she was able to get her legs under her, she wobbled to the nurse's station; the colors of the rainbow strobing before her eyes. She mustered up the strength to speak to the nurse at the window. "Sorry," she slurred, "something's come up—an emergency—I can't stay for my appointment today after all."

"Should we reschedule now?" The nurse said routinely, but reconsidered after noticing the pallor slowly creeping its way across Melissa's pained face. "Or we can give you a call?" She offered.

"Don't know." Melissa sputtered, leaning against the counter for support. "Got to go, now." She floated through the door like a phantom and promptly stumbled into the public restroom in the hallway. Melissa barfed up her anguish and disgust into the nasty toilet until her knees were shaking like jello.

CHAPTER 23

Golden Gate

"Money!" Melissa bellowed over her house phone. As usual, Douglas was missing in action, and she didn't much care who heard her. "You're not going to believe this!" She squalled.

"Calm down, Missy." Money tensed on his toothpick. "I can't hear you when you get up into them dog decibels—"

"I am so angry!" Melissa was sweating bullets. "I can barely breathe!"

"Are you sitting down?" Money cautioned.

"Wait." Melissa pulled her fuchsia-colored cashmere robe around her like a shield. "Okay," she mumbled, as she tried to settle herself on the suede couch in her beautifully sunlit Florida room, which overlooked her Olympic-sized swimming pool.

"Now, give it to me straight." Money soothed. "One word at a time."

"Okay." Melissa sucked in air. "I went to see Dr. Barrows today. Remember, I told you. He's the OB/GYN I've been going to, trying to get pregnant."

"Yep." Money flapped. "I'm with you so far…go 'head."

"Who do I run into…but Wanza Johnson-Grand!" She spat her name, one word at a time.

"Oh, no." Money sneered. "Don't tell me y'all share another man in common?"

"Not funny." Melissa barked. "I was shocked to my shoes when she came breezing out of his office for her annual and saw me sitting in the waiting room."

"Did she say anything?"

"Oh, yes!" Melissa steamed. "She was her usual smart-mouthed self. But this time she hit me with a bombshell from which I may never recover!"

"What?"

"Wanza told me…with wicked satisfaction…that Douglas…my own husband…has had…a vasectomy!"

"What? When?"

"Eight years ago…after his second son was born." Melissa raged. "And Wanza has known this all along…but Douglas never bothered to tell me!" She screeched. "All this time; all the hell I've put myself through trying to get pregnant—all the tests, the schedules, the needles; and every month, the devastating disappointment…and Douglas never told me that he can't father any more babies!" She broke down into heartbreaking sobs. "It was all I could do to save face with *Wanza-the-Witch*. It would just kill me if she knew I didn't know—"

"So Douglas had his li'l twinkie clipped, huh?" Money rumbled.

"Not funny, Money!" Melissa barked. "How can you joke about a thing like this?"

"You're right." Money tightened up on his toothpick. "So, how're you gonna tell him you know?"

"What?" Melissa flared. "I can't let on. I can't let Douglas know I know he's had a vasectomy."

"Huh?" Money slid his toothpick to one side. "He lied to you. I'd be all over his—"

"I can't call his hand like that, Money." Melissa trembled. "Then he'd have no reason to stay—"

"I don't get it—"

"He'd think our lovemaking was just a joke…if I knew I couldn't get pregnant."

"So what'll you do?"

"I'll keep making love to him…just like always—"

"So you think sex can hold a man?" Money snarled.

"But what else can I do—"

"Sex is one thing." Money fumed. "Marriage is another."

"How would you know?" Melissa ripped. "You've never been married—"

"But I'm a man!" Money blared. "Sex is a feeling. Marriage is a commitment, and yo' man Douglas ain't got one ounce of commitment in his entire soul," Money said with a twisted smirk. "Men like him think wives are meant to be cheated on while they get their just desserts on the side."

"So what can I do to keep us together?" Melissa pleaded.

"You're zooming him to get what you want. He's zooming you to get what he wants. But y'all ain't never been no *us*...'cause not one drop of honesty has ever passed between the two of you—"

"But, Money, I'm giving him all my love—"

"Lots of stuff passes itself off for love—"

"All the love in my heart—"

"And maybe that's more love than a man like him can stand." Money sighed. "Or maybe for once in your life, you're getting all nutty-brained 'cause this is the one man you can't wrap around your li'l finger—"

"But I need him, Money." Melissa whined.

"Tough, Missy!" Money sparked. "'Cause he only cares about his own needs."

"But I've done everything to keep him." Melissa pressed her point. "I gave up my career, my beliefs, my pride—" A tear caught in her throat. "I've given him all of me, Money. I've turned my life over to him—"

"Well, that is too much—"

"But I'm nearly 40, Money. I don't have time to start over with someone new. Douglas is my last chance for happiness. I can't afford to lose him...watch all my dreams go up in smoke—"

"What dreams?"

"I want a house full of cute kids; a shared life; a respected place in society; years and years of marital bliss—"

"Uggh!" Money flamed. "That's that *perfect-family* fairy-tale that Mother fed you. But wake up, Missy! This ain't no fairy tale. This is real life!"

"But—"

"You want what you want, but you get what you get." Money's jailhouse logic spewed over like an overheated volcano. "The sun rises. The sun sets. People make choices. And it has absolutely nothing to do with you, Missy. And no amount of doing on your part can change it. All you can do is deal with it…the way it is!"

"But how?" Melissa strained to understand his reasoning. "How?"

"Live your life, Missy." Money pleaded. "Do what's good for *you*. You can't *make* family—perfect or otherwise. And you can't make this marriage work by yourself!"

"But don't you understand—" Melissa broke down in piercing sobs. "I don't have a life—not without Douglas!"

CHAPTER 24
Gold Standard

"Hi, Pastor," Y whined pitifully, finding herself sitting in one of his guest chairs, again. "I wanna thank you for letting me talk to you today. I know I ain't been back to the church since you helped me get into the Center—"

"That's quite alright, Y." Pastor Meadows did his best to put her at ease, but unsure of her motives, he remained planted behind the piles of paperwork on his desk. Seeing her dressed in baggy jeans and a tee-shirt, however, he couldn't help but notice she wasn't any better off now than when he'd first laid eyes on her that Sunday morning. "I'm just happy to see you, again," he said genuinely. "What can I do for you?"

Y squirmed her skinny frame around in the chair until her tears broke loose. Her hair was longer, now, and she pushed the permed, corkscrew curls away from her face. She rubbed her eyes with the backs of her well-manicured hands as she squeaked out her agonizing story. "They're putting me out, Pastor—me and my kids!"

"What's that?" Pastor Meadows located his blue box and passed her a tissue.

"The folks at the Center...they say I got two weeks to find me another place 'cause I can't stay there no mo'."

"What happened, Y?" the pastor said patiently.

"I don't know!" She squawked. "I thought everything was just fine."

"That so?" Pastor Meadows knitted his thick, bushy brows.

"But it ain't fine...we're getting kicked out!"

"That so?" Pastor Meadows played along.

"Yeah!" Y exclaimed. "Them people been telling me I need to get my act together—go to school, get a job, take better care o' my kids. But I thought I had plenty time. And I thought I could—"

"String them along so you'd have somewhere safe and free to stay?" The pastor finished her thought.

"Yeah." Y nodded shamefully.

"But nothing's free, huh?" Pastor Meadows said quietly.

"Yeah." Y blubbered. "I saw all them other girls rushing 'round, trying to get stuff done. But I just wanted to chill-out in the video room, like it was with me and Larry Blow."

"Oh, I see." Pastor Meadows tensed. "And it looks like we're about to entertain ourselves right out of existence."

"But they ain't feeling me no mo', Pastor." Y sniveled. "They say they got rules, and me and my kids can't stay there—"

"So what're you going to do?"

"I begged them to let me stay just a little while longer." Y sobbed. "But they say I can't do in a few weeks what I haven't done in a whole year—"

"You've been there a year?"

"Yeah." Y sniffled. "I didn't realize it had been so long. But I guess I should o' figured it since Teesha's almost a year old." She twisted one of her curls around her finger. "And after a year, they say you either gotta be ready to move into your own apartment, or they take you outta their system for...uhh—"

"Failure to thrive." Pastor Meadows helped her out. "In fact, you got a bonus deal because they usually only give you six months to sink or swim."

"Really?" Y gaped.

"And I'm surprised you didn't know all this." Pastor Meadows got serious. "Because from what Wanza tells me, you said you had your caseworkers eating out of your hand—"

"I know, Pastor." Y whimpered. "But I was wrong—dead wrong. They gave me every chance to get myself together, but I...I just didn't take it. And now my po' kids are gonna suffer." She wailed, and her whole body began to tremble like a reed caught in a raging wind. "I messed up bad...real bad. And it ain't nobody's fault but mine—I was the one who lied; I was the one who was lazy; I was the one who tried every trick in the book; I—"

"Now-now." Pastor Meadows broke in on her tirade, giving her a moment to stem the tide of tears. And then he said quietly, "Jesus paid the price for every sin you could ever sin. Do you believe that, Y?"

"Huh?" Y accepted another tissue and dabbed at her eyes. "Well, my Granny did make me go to Sunday School when I was a kid. And, yeah, I always believed Jesus died on the cross for our sins; rose on the third day; and left this cruel world behind to go back to live with His Father in heaven."

"Is that so?" Pastor Meadows chuckled at her skillful recitation, which sounded like a first grader's catechism. "But do you believe Jesus died for *your* sins—the ones you've confessed to me, here, today."

"Well?" Y seriously considered the possibility. "Yeah, I believe Jesus died for my sins, too."

"So if you believe that, Y, your slate is wiped clean," Pastor Meadows declared.

"It is?"

"And do you believe that Jesus is Lord and has the right to call the shots in your life?"

"Now, I ain't always been able to buy into that one," Y said candidly, even though her hands were still shaking. "'Specially since Jesus ain't here no mo'—"

"Oh, I see." Pastor Meadow's anticipation waned.

"But I have been watching Miss Wanza live out what she believes in." Y quickly added. "'Cause when I first met her at this church, she was one, hot mess. But ever since she got saved, she been steady climbing…and I been steady falling back."

"Ever think the Lord may have allowed your circumstances so you can see how much you need Him?" Pastor Meadows eyed her carefully.

"No." Y sat up straighter and tuned-in more intently. It was obvious the pastor was going somewhere with this. "But I am starting to believe Jesus is alive in what goes on in the here-and-now." Y conceded. "Why, just look at how He's helping Miss Wanza."

"And do you believe that Jesus can make a difference in your life, too…if you let Him?"

Y dropped her head and the twitchiness in her body began to calm. "Never really thought about it, Pastor." She admitted. "Been too busy trying to fix things up for myself. But since you put it that way, yeah, I believe Jesus could make a difference in my life, too…if I let Him."

"Well, then." Pastor Meadows gleamed. "On the basis of your faith, we can start to pray about your situation—"

"Do you think Miss Wanza would take me back?" Y edged in. "'Cause I think I got it, now. I can't have nothing lessen I put something to it; right?" She sniffed. "I'll do better this time, Pastor. I promise. I'll listen. I'll—"

"First, let's you and me pray about it." Pastor Meadows took hold of her cold, clammy hands and helped her to her feet. "And then, maybe, we'll talk to Wanza."

CHAPTER 25
Golden Glimmer

"Pastor, you told me if I took Y back, you'd want a progress report in three months." Wanza lowered her new, slimmer figure into his guest chair with ease. It was a warm day in late September, but with fewer pounds, she didn't need her usual fan or her soda can. "So, here I am," she said.

"You're looking well, Sister Wanza," the pastor said, admiring her natural hair and the fresh glow that the attractive touch of makeup gave to her full lips and smooth, brown face, which had slimmed down to reveal her outstanding cheekbones. *Who knew she had such beauty hidden under those rainbow wigs and extra pounds? Now, I can see what Douglas must've seen in her. She's refreshingly honest, fiercely loyal, super smart...and down-right fine.* "Hrumph!" Pastor Meadows coughed away his naughty thought as though it were a frog in his throat. "Well, I guess Y isn't being too much trouble for you after all, huh?"

"No trouble at all, Pastor." Wanza smiled. "I know she's almost 20 years my junior, but she's like my little sister."

"That's good to hear."

"I had to quit volunteering over at the Center when my college classes started up in the summer." Wanza gave him a big grin. "But I hear from some of my old colleagues at the Center that they put the fear of God into Y when they put her out."

"Maybe." Pastor Meadows smirked. "But I'd like to think the Lord was wooing her to Himself after they put her out, because that's when she got saved.

"Guess you were right, Pastor." Wanza conceded. "Sometimes He puts us in a strain, so we'll have nowhere else to look, but up—"

"And if we keep our hands off of it," the pastor said, smiling, "He'll take over, too."

"Well, when I first went back to college this summer," Wanza said, "I never really considered how hard it would be when both me and the boys were in school in the fall." Wanza twisted her full mouth. "And let me tell you, it was about to get ugly."

"How so?"

"The boys are getting bigger; their classes are getting harder; and they're into sports, now. And I was having to haul them all over town and try to get my homework done, too." Wanza breathed. "Whew! It was getting really real, I tell you."

"So what's different now?" The pastor inquired.

"Y!" Wanza smiled. "When she got back to my house, that girl took over like a champ. She took up all the cooking and cleaning, and she got all the kids on a real good schedule. She can't help much with their homework. She didn't graduate from high school, you know. But she has everything else all lined up. So when I get home from my last class, all I have to do is help the boys with their homework and go to bed."

"So it's working well?"

"It's working splendidly." Wanza beamed. "I helped Y get her driver's license and leased her a little car, and she's taking the boys to all of their practices. And she's enjoying it, too."

"That's wonderful."

"Y's even learning to swim, so she can keep up with the boys when Ralph has them in the pool—"

"Who's Ralph?" Pastor Meadows' brows flung from side to side.

"Their private swim coach."

"Heated pool, too, I guess?"

"Yeah," Wanza said nonchalantly as though an in-home, Olympic-sized swimming pool was the most natural thing in the world.

"And what about Y's kids?" The pastor quizzed.

"Her little baby, Teesha, is such a joy; and you know, Austin, will be going to Pre-K, here, at the church next year. So we all get along real well."

"I'm proud to hear that." Pastor Meadows swelled. "After all you and Y have been through, I didn't know if it would work."

"Well, under normal circumstances, maybe it wouldn't." Wanza agreed. "We are both pretty headstrong, and we're light-years apart in many ways. But Y is also attending Bible Study with me here at the church, so it gives us some…common ground. We have something to discuss together, and we both agree that no matter how we feel, the Lord's way is right. So when we start *being ourselves* and messing up." Wanza worked her neck. "We're always trying to get back to center…if you know what I mean."

"I know exactly what you mean." Pastor Meadows nodded. "Me and Candi have been married a lot of years, but we are two, very different people. And the Lord's word is what keeps getting us back to center every day."

"And when the kids see us trying to get along, they get along that much better."

"You two are a great example." The pastor commended.

"I've also been talking to Y about getting her GED," Wanza said. "You know she needs that and more to make it in this world, especially when she goes solo." Wanza shrugged. "I'm on her team and all, but she realizes she can't always stay up under me. But with all that's going on right now, she's decided to wait until I graduate to pursue it."

"And when's that?"

"Oh! I didn't tell you; did I, Pastor?" Wanza beamed. "Since I only needed 60 credit hours, I'll be a college graduate as of March, 2016…right after my 40th birthday!"

"Wow! I'm so happy for you, Wanza!" Pastor Meadows said, antsy with excitement. "What then?"

"Oh, I don't know." Wanza considered thoughtfully. "I'm majoring in Sociology and Family Development...so I want to do something to help families...children...young women like Y and her kids. But I'm still praying about it, and we'll see what doors the Lord opens for me."

"Now, that's the Spirit!" Pastor Meadows rejoiced.

"Know what, Pastor?" Wanza's voice mellowed like that of a small child's.

"What's that?" The pastor braced himself.

"I'm so glad I forgave Douglas." Wanza shook both of her hands freely and turned them palms up, just as the pastor had once done for her. "I wouldn't have gotten any of this good stuff...if he hadn't left me."

"Sometimes we want things fixed." Pastor Meadows smiled at her growing level of maturity. "But the Lord wants them changed—"

"I'm gone!" Wanza gathered up her things and headed for the door. 'I've taken up enough of your time."

"Give my best to Y and the kids." Pastor Meadows waved. "And hope to see you on Sunday."

"For sure, Pastor." Wanza strutted out of the door; head held high. "For sure!"

CHAPTER 26

Flaming Gold

"WHAT-THE-WHAT!!" Douglas yelled as Melissa shrank like a finger-puppet into his over-sized office. His booming voice was vibrating the platinum records on his vanity wall. Melissa had figured something was up when his assistant issued the summons for her to report. The sizzle in Charlotte's voice was sparking with animosity when she commanded, "The boss wants to see you—ASAP!"

"What's the matter, Babe." Melissa whispered and slid into one of the red leather side chairs.

"What's the matter, Babe?" Douglas mocked her little girl's voice. "How can you come into my presence...a principal in my company...asking me what's the matter?"

"Why're you so angry, Douglas?" Melissa chanced a look in his direction.

"Okay." Douglas' handsome nostrils flared. "If we're gonna play 20-questions, let's get to it." He drummed his fingers against his massive desk. "Did your late filing of D-Bomb's, 2-Tight's, and four other's tax returns cost these guys over a million dollars?"

"But—"

"Before you say another word, Melissa, think!" Douglas roared. "Cause I don't want to hear anything but truth come out of your mouth from this point forward. No gimmicks. No tricks. No lies. Just answer my question!"

"Well...yes." Melissa squirmed. "But—"

"No buts, Melissa!" Douglas blared. "Do you know what you've done?"

"But I've got calls in to some of my old colleagues at the IRS. We can straighten this out." Melissa pleaded. "This was just an oversight on the part of my staff—"

"That's not how I heard it, Melissa." Douglas' voice poked into her like a sharp stick. "The way I hear it is your staff had the proper papers prepared and tagged for your signature days ago...but they just sat there on your desk, unsigned, past the final negotiated deadline."

"I know." Melissa fumbled. "But I've been so busy—"

"Are you kidding me?" Douglas hooted. "That's your excuse for costing my clients their hard-earned dollars—you've been too busy!"

"Lower your voice, Douglas." Melissa squirmed. "The whole office will hear—"

"I don't care who hears!" Douglas squalled like a bird of prey. "You'd better be glad I don't come 'cross this desk and grab you by your throat!"

"Douglas!"

"Appearances!" Douglas screamed. "That's all you ever care about...keeping up appearances—at the office, at church, at home." He pierced her with a diabolical stare. "But you see, my dear, this business is *mine*. These clients are *mine*. This office is *mine*. That house you park your lovely carcass in is *mine*. So what're you bringing to the table, huh?" He blistered out his own response. "Nothing! 'Cause I can get sex when I can't eat!"

"But I—"

"Instead of adding real value around here, you've been pouting at the office and at home." Douglas blistered off his list of grievances. "You're upset because you can't get pregnant, and you don't know why. You're upset because you have to work with people you think are beneath you, but who just happen to pay our bills. You're upset because you're sneaking up on 40, and you haven't pulled-off what you set out to accomplish. You're upset because you can't have your way with me, and you're used to casting every man under your spell. You're upset. You're tired. You're losing sleep…and your looks are going south!" Douglas drew attention to her sunken eyes, limp hair, and the designer clothes that were hanging loosely on her skinny frame. "Does that just about sum it up for you, Miss Melissa?" His face contorted into an anger mass, and his chair whirled around violently when he hopped up.

Melissa drew back from him in fright. "But Douglas, I'm your wife." She sniveled. "And I feel like I'm all alone. You're never home. You never give me your support. Sometimes I don't even know if I'm going or coming." She strained to hold onto some shred of dignity. "But I assure you, this oversight was not intentional—"

"Do you want to know what your *unintentional* oversight has cost me?" Douglas didn't wait for her to answer. "D-Bomb, 2-Tight and one of the other guys—that you refuse to acknowledge as necessary human beings—are the opening act for my mega concert! We've been pumping the media that they'll be headlining the show, and everybody is wild to see them." Douglas flung his hands over his head. "But because of your *unintentional* oversight, Melissa, they say they're backing out of the concert. They say, 'We don't wanna work with a skirt who straight-up lies to us; won't give us our props; skims off our bankroll; and who ain't down with us!'" Douglas seethed. "And if they back out of my concert, we'll lose millions. Not to mention, I'll never be able to show my face in this industry, again. If I can't get my own stable to back me in the biggest, single endeavor of my life, who am I? And you'd better believe word of this screw-up will get around, and the egg will be on my face, Melissa. Not yours! Mine!"

"But I'm trying to make it right, Douglas." Melissa fumbled for words. "I've got calls in to some people who owe me favors. And I promise you, this will never, ever, happen, again—"

"Oh, I know it won't!" Douglas blared, without a moment's hesitation. "Because you and your entire staff are fired!" He roared. "I've moved in Burn & Burn Associates to clean-up your mess and to handle things *professionally* from here on out—"

"But Douglas, I've been trying my best…living outside myself to get along with your clients…trying to give this thing 110%...to look out for us—"

"And maybe that's where you made your mistake, Melissa." Douglas wailed. "Because I've been giving it a 110%...to look out for me!"

"But we're a team—"

"Save your breath, Slick." Douglas thumbed her to the door. "You're outta here! And don't you bother going back to *my* house. I don't want to see you there, either!"

"But Douglas," Melissa stammered; her voice barely audible. "Where will I go?"

"Go hang out with your jail-bird brother." Douglas glared at her indignantly. "You two don't have to keep your secrets from me any longer—"

"Wh-at?"

"I'm a businessman, Melissa. Did you think I'd marry you without thoroughly vetting you *and* your entire family?" Douglas' chiseled face hardened. "Yeah, I know Money is a two-time loser and a recovering drug addict. I know he has a passion for rum. And I know you got him out on parole this time, and you put him up in that flea-bag, flop-house downtown and got him a janitor's job. And I know you've been sneaking into my bank account, too. You've been giving away my hard-earned cash to your con-brother. And you never thought, not once, to discuss it with me first. Did you think I wouldn't know?" Douglas' face turned a violent shade of purple. "Really?"

"But—"

"Get out, Melissa, before I really lose my temper!" Douglas glared at her with eyes ablaze. "I've gotta clean-up your mess and get my concert back on track before I lose my shirt *and* my reputation." He blistered. "Get out o' my sight this minute, Woman! Ge-t! Ou-t!"

Melissa slunk out of his office like a jangling marionette and closed the door behind her. She pretended not to notice the look of sympathy scrawled across Charlotte's stricken face.

Well, I hope I didn't overplay my hand. Douglas snickered to himself when his door closed. *If I can get at Miss Redd, I'll have Melissa running for the hills. But...if not...well...I do need somebody at home to satisfy my urges.*

CHAPTER 27
Golden Embers

Despite her trembling knees and foggy brain, Melissa somehow managed to make her way to the Howlin' Moon Blues Café against the noon-rush traffic. Money had promised to meet her there when he heard her pitiful state over the phone. She was seated in a booth for two near the rear window, shivering, when he arrived twenty minutes later.

"Hi, Money." Melissa whimpered.

"Hi, yourself." Money gnawed away on his toothpick when he saw her swollen eyes, tremors and disheveled appearance. "You alright there, Missy?" He eased into their booth.

"I've had better days." She raised her chin bravely.

"I got here as quick as I could—"

"Thanks, Money," Melissa said breathlessly. "I can always depend on you."

Money let the waiter come and go before he pursued it. "So what happened?"

"Douglas…he kicked me out of his office today, Money." She battled back her tears. "For good—"

"But why?" Money soothed.

"We made a mistake—" Her words caught in her throat. "I made a mistake…and for that he ridiculed me in front of the entire staff and literally threw me out of his office—"

"That low-down—" Money rose up out of his seat, set on seeking revenge, but Melissa held onto his hardened fists to prevent his departure.

"Sit down, Money, please." She implored. "I'm alright, now."

"But he had no right—"

"He's just under a lot of pressure." Melissa countered. "This blasted mega concert has him going out of his mind with worry. It's less than six months away, you know, and there're so many loose ends—"

"That's no excuse—"

"And I'm not much better." Melissa defended. "Every time I need him, he's away in Europe, or off God-knows-where-doing-God-knows-what with that Willamina Redd." She tilted back her head so her tears wouldn't show in public. "All I do is work, work, work with his hoodlum clientele and go home to an empty house every night. It's making me crazy, too!"

"Do you think Miss Redd's moving in on your territory?" Money twirled his toothpick.

"I don't know." Melissa pouted. "She acts all innocent with me on Sunday mornings at True Vine; speaks to me all sweet and respectful, like I'm the *older* one. But I'm not that much older than her—" Melissa caught herself rambling. "But who knows?"

"Yeah—"

"But it's that mega concert that has him all spun up." Melissa expounded. "It'll be live and showcased all over the world. There can be no slip-ups—none. Douglas is putting all of his eggs in this one basket, and it's turning him into a monster—"

"Or maybe…he's just moving on to something he likes better—"

"I refuse to think that way, Money." Melissa jutted out her chin in stiff defiance. "It's hard. But I'm going to stay strong and stand by my man until he works his way through this…just like Mother would—"

"You think Mother was strong?" Money's nose flared. "I think she was a weak, clingy individual who used her man to get what she wanted—to secure her status in Knoxville society so people would have to look up to her. She came straight outta the Knoxville projects, and she never wanted to go back—no matter who she had to step on to do it."

"Money, don't say that—"

"And all those years you were her li'l angel…her own…*good-wife-in-training*—"

"Money!"

"Did I ever tell you how our precious Mother died?" Money took a sharp, tasteless bite into his thick cheeseburger.

"How would you know?" Melissa slashed at him. "I had to go to Mother's funeral in 2013—alone. Because, if you'll remember, you were back in jail…for the second time!"

"And what did they tell you?"

"That Mother had a massive heart attack and died on the spot." Melissa recounted. "And the service was beautiful…four years to the day after President Obama had graced our church…and just one month after his second, magnificent inauguration. There were so many dignitaries at Mother's funeral and so many beautiful, fragrant flowers from all over—even as far as the White House—"

"You're right." Money gritted on his toothpick. "I was in jail…for the second time. But I know how Mother really died, because as soon as I stepped outta the State Pen, Mother Whatnot summoned me over to her house for a li'l meet." His throat tightened as though the old woman were channeling her voice through his tortured mind. "Mother Whatnot." He croaked. "She told me the *rest* of the story—"

****

"'You see, Son,' Mother Whatnot said to me that day, nearly dragging me by my ear into her tiny kitchen. She wasn't satisfied 'til she'd settled me down at her table with a hot cup of tea and some of them nasty tea cakes. Yuck!"

"'I know you was in prison when yo' mama died.' Her li'l gnarled hands patted mine. 'And there's gonna be a lot of whispers and looks when you go back to Faith Freewill,' she said, 'and you ain't gonna understand none o' that. So that's why I brought you over here today. I'm gonna tell you...once and for all...how it was yo' mama came to die, so them folk don't have nothing to hold over you.'"

"Mother Whatnot drew me close with a whisper and said, 'You see, when they pulled the dirt over yo' daddy, it wasn't long 'fore the Trustees formed a search committee for a new pastor. Yo' mama was in mourning, but you best believe she kept a close eye on the situation. Every time they'd interview a seasoned pastor, somehow or another, yo' mama would put a monkey wrench in that thang. She didn't want no mature pastor, who know'd what he was doing, to have nothing to do with Faith Freewill. But finally, along and along, they came up with this nice couple—young preacher and his sweet wife—Pastor and Sister Strong. That seemed to set well with yo' mama 'cause I figure she thought she'd have a better chance o' keeping them in line and telling them what to do.'"

"About that time, Mother Whatnot tossed her head back and gave out a little hoot. 'But what she didn't count on was that young man is full of the Holy Ghost, I tell you. He can preach. He can teach. It was so the young folk were flocking to Faith Freewill, and the old folk were listening to what this mighty, young preacher had to say...some of 'em prob'ly hearing the Gospel for the very first time. And since he was so full o' fire, everybody gave his young wife their respect, too.' Mother Whatnot grinned and showed me her snaggled teeth. 'She's a pretty, timid little thing, but she can sing like a songbird and play that keyboard like her hands got wings. It was like the church was having its own private Pentecost, and Pastor Strong was becoming the talk o' the town! And if I tell you all this didn't make yo' mamma madder than a hornet, Son, I'd be telling you a lie.' Mother Whatnot pinned me with her li'l beady eyes. 'But anyhow,' she said, 'this all happened while you was behind bars. But don't you go feeling no way bad 'bout that. The Lord don't save perfect people. He calls the people who ain't perfect and are willing to admit it.' She winked. 'Pastor Strong taught us that.'"

"When Mother Whatnot grinned, again, I had to look away from her messed-up mouth, but that didn't stop her. 'So anyhow,' she went on to say, 'some of the Deacons took it upon themselves to ask yo' mama off the front row. I think they was just jugging at her, but they said that row was reserved for the Pastor's family 'cause, from time to time, the First Lady's mama and sister would come to visit with her. And that's where they wanted them to sit. Her sister is a real looker, you know, and them devilish deacons just prob'ly wanted a chance to look at her legs. But that made yo' mama hotter than a .38-caliber bullet!'"

"And that's when Mother Whatnot started bobbing back and forth in her kitchen chair like it had rockers. She said, 'Yo' mama had the Trustees call a special meeting to take up the matter. They tell me she came to that meeting loaded for bear. She was dressed to the nines in all the minks and diamonds she had in her closet. And she told 'em, "My husband is the Senior Pastor Emeritus of this church, and as such, I expect the respect and honor due my station." They say she said, "I still have a host of supporters in this church, and I am not going to give way to any other First Lady, especially one who's half my age and hasn't a clue about how to run church business. And if you want a church fight, I'll give you a church fight!" And about that time they tell me yo' mama's mouth flared open; her eyes rolled back up in her head; she grabbed hold o' her throat and fell out—dead—right there on the spot.'"

"Then Mother Whatnot pinned her lil' beady eyes on me and said, 'I know you must feel some kind o' way…losing yo' parents so close together like that. And I believe in many ways yo' mama was real sincere. But sometimes, we can be sincerely wrong. And I tell you the truth; since she's been gone, folk have started putting their eyes on Jesus, and the church has been humming along even stronger ever since. Which just goes to show what I've been trying to tell you, Son.' She sucked on her missing teeth. 'You got to know Jesus for yo'self.'"

★★★★★★★★★★★★

"I didn't go back to Faith Freewill after my meet with Mother Whatnot. What was the use?" Money brought his attention back to the present. "And thanks to you sponsoring my parole, Missy, I didn't have to stay in Knoxville. I came straight up to Nashville, after that."

"And I'm real glad you did." Melissa reached for her brother's hands with the benefit of fresh eyes. His needle scars, prison tats, and slick ways were starting to make more sense to her, now. For so many years, he'd been saddled with his super-hero complex, trying to bolster her self-esteem and protect her from the pain and humiliation of their scandalous family secrets—and no one was the wiser.

"Tell me Mother Whatnot died not long after that." Money mused. "And from what I heard, everybody was running 'round trying to spin a yarn about their blessed connection to the dearly departed; even though, the woman's life and death had nothing to do with them." He snorted. "All we could do is love her, and most of us didn't even do that—" Money stopped mid-sentence and rolled his tears back up his cheeks. "But she was the only one of 'em that ever loved me…and the love people leave behind…well…it lives on—"

"I'm sorry for every mean thing I ever said about her, too." Melissa sniffed. "And I'm totally devastated by what happened to Mother…but all the more reason for us to stick together, now,

Money. In fact, I need you more than ever." She forced some sunshine into her voice. "We're the last of the Mighty Manns!"

"Yes, we are!" Money twirled his toothpick like a twizzle stick. "So quit getting all nutty-brained 'bout this stuff and take life as it comes," he said. "That's what I had to learn in lock-up."

"I will." Melissa nodded slowly.

"So…you gonna get a hotel room for the night?" Money pushed back his half-eaten burger, which was starting to gag in his throat.

"No." Melissa's voice sagged. "I'm going home—"

"Home? But he don't care 'bout you, Missy!" Money's voice spiked over the drone of the noisy café. "You've gotta care 'bout you!"

"He does care!" Melissa retorted. "His priorities are just a little confused right now—"

"Okay, I hear ya." Money worked at mellowing his tone. "But you can't let this man take over yo' life—"

"What do you know about it, Money?" Melissa protested. "You've never been in love!"

"I love you!" Money's voice quivered with bottled-up anger. "And I can't stand what you're letting this joker do to you…in the name o' love—"

"But it'll be alright, Money; really, it will." Melissa squeezed her brother's throbbing fists. "Despite all his noise," she said confidently, "Douglas would be devastated if I wasn't there when he got home. It's just the pressure of this mega concert. It's driving him nuts!"

"Okay, Missy," Money said warily, patting her outstretched hand. "But if you need Ole-Money—for anything—you call me—"

"I will, Big Brother." Melissa whimpered. "I will."

CHAPTER 28

Golden Trophy

"Well, the holidays are over." Pastor Meadows announced as the women got settled in his study. "And we're off to a fresh start in 2016!" However, it wasn't apparent by the usual clutter that was littering his desktop.

"You got that right," Wanza said, as she settled into one of the guest chairs at his desk. She was looking quite the professional in her tailored, tweed suit and navy pumps. "Everything is picking up, again."

"Um-hmm." Y echoed as she sat down in the chair alongside her. Her hair was bone straight and parted in the center, and she was wearing a pretty red sweater, jeggings and fringed suede boots. Pastor Meadows was quite pleased with her transformation.

"Hope you had a great holiday season." The pastor continued.

"We did." Y offered. "Me and the kids had a good-ole-time decorating and cooking and such, while Miss Wanza finished up her finals and class papers. It was awesome!"

"Glad to hear that," Pastor Meadows said. "Me and Candi passed a quiet time, and we were very grateful for the break."

"But you're right, Pastor," Wanza chatted on. "It is a new day."

"And that's why I wanted to meet with you ladies, today." Pastor Meadows's leather chair creaked as he shifted his broad frame to draw closer to them.

"What's that?" Wanza spouted.

"There's something that's been troubling me that I want us as a church family to address." He confided. "And me and Candi have been mulling it over for some time.

"What might that be?" Y tooted.

"I've been watching young women with small children come through here on their way to one agency or the other." He gave Y a comforting glance. "Make no mistake," he said, "you're only one of a hundred we've tried to help."

"I know." Y shifted self-consciously.

"And it seems the same story plays itself out over and over, again," Pastor Meadows said. "The young ladies get in some kind of need or trouble. They come to the church or an agency for help. They get placed in facilities and are offered resources of varying kinds to turn their lives around—education, food, housing, on and on. But for some unknown reason, with very few exceptions, it rarely seems to do the trick. The women and their children seem not that much better off, and they continue to stay in need of varying degrees. With all of our good intentions, nothing ever seems to break the cycle—"

"Uh-huh." Y intoned.

"And, maybe, I'm just not seeing it right." The pastor threw up his heavy hands. "I'm no woman, and I've not walked a mile in their shoes." His bushy brows twisted in concern. "But I've watched you two, and I've seen how much you've grown. And I just wanted us to have this sit-down today so you can help me understand this whole phenomenon a little better."

"Whatever we can do, Pastor." Wanza nodded.

"I don't know." Pastor Meadows continued. "Maybe it's just that these young ladies have had a hard road—"

"I came up hard, too." Wanza inserted. "That's no excuse. My mother, Wanda, was a single mother, and it was eight of us—"

"Wow!" Y chortled. "Bet y'all had fun fighting over the last slice o' bologna, huh?"

"My oldest brother and I are by the same daddy." Wanza disclosed, ignoring Y's smart-mouthed remark. "But our Dad got killed in a car crash two weeks before he was set to marry Mama."

She shrugged. "Guess she just gave up after that because all the rest of the kids have different daddies—"

Wanza shutdown, but Pastor Meadows beckoned for her to continue. "Well, we moved around North Nashville from one cheap apartment to the other; one baby-daddy to the other, but nothing ever stuck." Wanza smirked. "Some of Mama's boyfriends weren't so bad...some of them were just downright mean...and some of them...well...let's just say...I ended up having to dodge all of them for one reason or the other." She lifted up her chin to stave off her tears when she remembered fighting off a grown man's groping hands. "And then Mama died, and all the children scattered. Me and my oldest brother keep in touch; but the others, not so much. And maybe...that's why I fell so hard for Douglas. Because he represented stability...something I'd never had." She rustled. "So don't tell me about these women having it hard—"

"As long as you think life is 'bout getting over, getting by, gaming the weak and stupid," Y said, tooting out her lips, "you ain't never gonna change."

"So you agree with Mrs. Lawson down at the Center?" Pastor Meadows knitted his bushy brows. "She says these young women are going nowhere fast because they haven't made it up in their own minds what they want to do with their lives. She preaches it to me all the time: 'We can give them the resources, but without an object in view, without a goal in mind for themselves and their children, it's like having a roadmap without a destination; like having the words without the music. So they go from handout to handout, getting by until the next time they have a need. It's just a revolving door.'"

"Yup...she right." Y's lip quivered, recalling her time at the Center. "I was trying to get three-hots-and-a-cot—for free—just doing enough not to get kicked outta the program. But I wasn't trying to build no kind o' life for me and my kids. I wasn't even thinking that far—"

149

"I think it's just that they don't see how much God loves them." Wanza added. "Growing up, I didn't care much about being at the church-house, or dealing with church folk and all their mess. I thought it was just one, big waste of time." She smiled. "But, now, I realize being *at* church doesn't matter…because it's not about all the fine buildings or the drama. The church…is the people who've put their personal faith *in* Jesus Christ…and He, in turn, puts His Holy Spirit *in* us. And His church is always alive and well—"

"You got that right!" Y hooted.

"And when He became my Number-One," Wanza said, finishing her thought in spite of Y's worrisome interruptions, "everything and everybody just seemed to fall into place."

"I agree." The pastor folded his arms across his broad chest. "The Lord wants us to have one faith—in Him; one hope—in Him; and one love—from Him—"

"And any love we happen to get from people along the way is just *hot* gravy." Y grinned as she repeated what she'd heard the pastor say so many times from the pulpit.

"Um-hmm." Pastor Meadows smiled; pleased that Y had actually been listening to his sermons. "We love people out of the heart of love that Jesus gives to us, not expecting anything from them in return—"

"Because our lives *belong* to the Lord." Wanza piped in with another one of the pastor's well-worn homilies. "And we walk *alongside* people."

"Then, I guess, we're in agreement." The pastor clasped his strong hands together. He was so elated with the progress of these two ladies he had to resist the urge to give each one of them a fist-bump. "It's no wonder none of these programs have any lasting impact on the problems because they're all like putting a band aid on an open wound. But the wound has to heal from the inside-out in order for the band aid to work."

"Yeah." Y pursed her lips. "And we gotta stop looking at folk as a chance to get over, and start seeing folk as a chance to give back…and then we'll get ours. Life's a big circle like that." Y sniffed. "'Cause if we don't give back, we be like…a tick on a dog; like killing the goose that lays the golden egg—"

"Y!" Wanza finally broke in on her friend's rant, unable to endure it another moment. "Where do you come up with all this stuff?"

"What?" Y shrugged. "I had a Granny, and all that stuff she used to tell me is starting to make some sense—"

"But you're right, Pastor." Wanza threw Y the side-eye to keep her quiet. "People have to change on the inside before anything can change on the outside."

"And only the Spirit of the Lord has the power to change us on the inside." Pastor Meadows concluded. "So, you see, I've been thinking we need to do more than just ship these young women off to agencies—"

"But what can we do?" Wanza puzzled.

"We've got to organize a ministry around these young women and their children," Pastor Meadows said. "We've got to introduce them to Jesus." And then they can take the resources they're given and build a productive life for themselves and their families."

"But how can it work, Pastor?" Wanza flapped. "Some folk can be as close to the Word as a kiss on the cheek and still not change. Remember Judas—"

"And Mr. Douglas?" Y snickered.

"Yes, but it's not our role to judge, ladies." The pastor corrected. "Our only mission is to share the Gospel, so that people have a choice. The outcome is in the Lord's hands…and growth takes time—"

"Well, if time is money, Pastor, you're gonna need plenty of it." Y teased. "Cause to change the hearts and minds of the chick-a-dees I know and love, it's gonna take plenty o' time."

"Well, not to put too fine a point to it," Pastor Meadows said, "Sister Willamina Redd has given a sizeable offering to get this new ministry off the ground. And she's talking it up with her friends in the music business. And I'm sure we'll have other members of the church, who have a heart for what we're doing, who'll step forward, as well—"

"That Willamina Redd is the real deal!" Wanza chimed in. "She took me to Dallas-Fort Worth to see one of her gigs—all expenses paid—just because I told her I'd always dreamed of seeing the inside of one of those honky-tonks."

"She did?" Pastor Meadows' brows twitched.

"Yes, indeed!" Wanza bragged. "And, boy, did we have fun— rode the mechanical bull; checked out all the hot spots; hung out with her musician friends; stayed in the finest hotel." Wanza's smile grew wider as she recalled the fun she'd had. "And not only is Willamina one of the nicest people in the world, that young lady's got some serious talent. She can sho-nuff sing! And everybody just loves her!"

"Well, I'm happy to hear that." Pastor Meadows nodded. "Glad to know you've made fast friends."

"So how'd Willamina come to know about your dream, Pastor?" Wanza inquired. "Did you contact her?"

"No." Pastor Meadows confided. "Actually, she came to me asking what ministry she could get involved in given the limited time she has to offer. I gave her the broad brush of my idea, and she was all for it. Sister Redd has a heart for single-parent households since she grew up in one herself. And she realizes how difficult the road can be."

"So…how do we get started?" Wanza said excitedly. "No time like the present; right?"

"Absolutely!" Pastor Meadows clasped his strong hands. "I see both you and Y as a model of what the Lord can do with a converted heart and a willingness to change. You've been practicing what the Bible teaches, and your progress has been phenomenal in just a few months."

"Ahh!" Y smiled shyly. "You really think so, Pastor?"

"I know so." Pastor Meadows contended. "You two have a testimony that needs to be shared and duplicated, over and over, again."

"Then, next steps!" Wanza blared, like the professional social scientist she was studying to be. "When do we kick it off?"

"The next step, as you so aptly put it," Pastor Meadows said, "is for you to consent to becoming the Director of the newest ministry at True Vine—"

"Whaaat?" Wanza nearly fainted dead away. "Me?" Her eyes were wide open, and she covered her mouth with both hands. "But what're you saying, Pastor?"

"I'm saying your degree from TSU is just a few months away." He ticked off his points on his stubby fingers. "You'll have a degree in Sociology and Family Development with a minor in Business. You are a member of True Vine. You can afford to work for peanuts until we get this ministry off the ground because you have your own independent source of income." He thumbed at Y. "Besides, you have a trusty side-kick, over here, who can't only continue to help you at home until you get your feet under you, but she can also get her GED and be your assistant right here in the ministry—"

"Stop! Stop!" Wanza was fishing for air. "You're taking me by storm."

"Not me," the pastor said. "This is the Lord's doing...and it's marvelous before our eyes." He grinned. "You're equipped to do it. You can do it. And if you want to do it...then it's heaven-sent."

"But what will we call the new ministry?" Y said excitedly. "'Cause I know Miss Wanza can do it...with the Lord's help...and I'm sure willing to pitch in."

"I don't know." Pastor Meadows furrowed his bushy brows. "The name of the new ministry...hmm...I'll leave that up to our new Director to decide."

CHAPTER 29

Gold Bars

"Missy," Money whispered over his pay-by-the-minute tracfone."

"What?" Melissa put her house phone on speaker, and the sound reverberated against the empty walls. As usual, Douglas was missing in action; and besides, she just didn't much care anymore. "Speak up, Money. I can't hear you."

"I'm in trouble, Missy—"

"What kind of trouble?" Melissa cinched the waist on her lounging pajamas to keep herself warm. An unexpected, February frost had etched an icy pattern on the windows in her lovely Florida room.

"The cops are looking for me." Money's voice trembled.

"Looking for you?" Melissa squawked. "For what?"

"Murder." Money's voice cratered.

"Murder!" Melissa screeched.

"It's not what you think, Missy." Money's words popped like hot grease. "Sure, I knew the guy. I had a beef with the guy. But, no, I did not murder the guy—"

"Who is he?"

"He was a pimp who plied his trade in the back alley near my janitor's job." Money hammered. "And sure, we may've had a difference of opinion over one o' his girls. But I did not murder the guy—"

"So why do the police think you did?" Melissa could feel the pressure mounting, and the throbbing in her temples was beginning to give her a blinding headache. She managed to flop onto the couch before she fell backwards.

"I dunno." Money mumbled. "But I spied the cops hanging outside my apartment...and one o' my pals says they're looking to jam me up with this thang."

"Where're you now?" Melissa braced herself.

"Hiding out." Money clamped down on his toothpick. "Better you don't know where. Shouldn't even be calling you on your line...but I need your help, Missy—"

"Help with what?" Melissa wailed as she massaged her aching temples. "You're stressing me out, here. You're killing me, Money—"

"Don't worry." Money reassured her. "I don't want you to get involved...but I do need a favor."

"What, Money? What?"

"Well, you see...I've got my stash on me—"

"Your stash?" Melissa freaked. "You're not supposed to have a stash!"

"I know...but...see...I do." Money's voice ran the scale from groaning to begging. "And I can't afford to get caught holding if the cops ever catch up with me. I just can't, Missy. I'm a two-time loser—"

"I know. I know—"

"But I didn't do no murder." Money groveled. "I swear. But I can't get caught holding—"

"So what do you want me to do? What?"

"I'm gonna swing by your house when it gets dark. I'll hide my stash behind our secret door on your porch. You don't have to do a thing. Okay?"

"I don't know, Money." Melissa flinched. "What is it?"

"Nothing major." Money swore. "Just some...lightweight painkillers and such. But I can't have 'em on me, okay?"

"Let me think." Melissa took a moment to breathe. "Well, okay, Money…if you think there's no other way. But I don't want to know when you come or when you go. Is that clear?"

"Sure, Missy. Sure thing." Money twirled his toothpick from side to side. "I'll drop if off and nobody'll be the wiser—"

"I can't take much more of this, Money!" Melissa flailed her hands in the air like a mad woman. "I'm already dealing with one crazy man…Douglas and his mega-concert-from-hell is only three months away. I do not need you to get picked up by the police, Money. We do not need any negative publicity, right now. I cannot have you messing up Douglas' concert. Do you hear me, Money? Do not get picked up by the police! Do not—"

"Not if I can help it!" Money snarled back at her. "'Cause I didn't do no murder. I swear!"

CHAPTER 30
Gold Dust

Nearly two months had passed since Melissa had heard from Money. She was biting her nails down to the quick with worry, waiting to hear that he was safe. Even the brand-new, red Mercedes convertible that Douglas had surprised her with over the holidays as a peace offering couldn't ease the pain. She didn't dare leave home in her snazzy, new ride for fear of missing one of Money's calls. She felt as nervous and jumpy as an overdue expectant mother. However, Douglas hadn't even noticed her agitated state because their shared dwelling was more like a cold-war zone than a home. They were like two ships passing on a long, artic night with no port in sight.

More out than in, Douglas' excuse was he was busy putting the finishing touches on his mega concert. But Melissa had no way of knowing if that were true because all of her privileges and access at his headquarters building had been cutoff when he kicked her out of his office. Even on the rare occasions when Douglas reached for her deep into the night, their attempts at lovemaking were awkward and dispassionate, lacking sufficient fire to thaw the mounting iceberg.

The strain was becoming more than Melissa could handle when the telephone in her Florida room finally rang. "Missy, you gotta help me!" Money sniveled over the pay phone, without giving her a chance to answer.

"Money!" Melissa tensed, fear trailing down her armpits like giant goosebumps. "Where in the world are you? I've been so worried—"

"Downtown...in a holding cell...2nd Precinct—"

"Holding cell!" Melissa lost it. Her shrill screams carried over the whole house. "You're in jail...again?"

"Yeah, I'm in jail." Money whimpered. "I tried my best to dodge the po-po, but them jokers hunted me down like a rabbit. But, Missy-Missy-Missy, I didn't do no murder—"

"That's what you keep saying, Money!" Melissa yelped. "But, nonetheless, you're under arrest at the 2nd Precinct! I thought you were hiding out—"

"I need you to get me a lawyer, Missy…real bad."

"Why do you need a lawyer if you didn't do it, Money?" Melissa sizzled.

"Uh-h…there's been a lineup." Money slowed. "And eyewitnesses showed up—"

"And—" Melissa prompted.

"And…two of the eyewitness picked me outta the lineup…they say I'm the guy—"

"What?" Melissa flared. "But, Money, you said you didn't do it—"

"I didn't do no murder, Missy." Money repeated. "I swear."

"Then why did the eyewitnesses pick you out of the lineup?"

"Dunno." Money groaned. "I been in that back alley where they found the body lots o' times. My janitor's job is near there." He stammered. "Maybe, they just seen me with that dude before and got confused or something…I don't know."

"Sure." Melissa clipped sharply.

"It's a bogus bust, Missy. I swear." Money pleaded.

"You swore to me last time you didn't do it." Melissa burned. "But you did…and you got your second strike to prove it—"

"I know." Money's voice pained with remorse. "I lied to you that time, Missy. But I did not do this…not this time. And I need a good lawyer. And I need him pretty quick—"

"This will be your third strike, Money—"

"This is a capital murder charge, Missy. They could put me away for life on this bum rap…or give me the needle." Money ramped up his plea. "And you don't know what kind o' stuff these cops'll do to a two-time loser when they get me hemmed up behind these iron bars. So I need a lawyer...a good one...quick!"

"How much?"

"I don't know." Money quibbled. "But if I can get out on bond, it'll probably be ten or twenty—"

"Thousand dollars?" Melissa yelped. "I don't have that kind of money. I don't even have a job, now; remember?"

"I know, Missy." Money's voice broke. "But can you get it?"

"I'd have to ask Douglas." Melissa whimpered.

"Then can you ask him?" Money wrestled with his pride. "Just this one time...for me?"

"Oh, Money." Melissa's heart sank at the enormity of her situation. "Do you know what this means? Douglas will absolutely freak if this bad news hits the press right before his mega concert—"

"I didn't do no murder, Missy," Money said, feeling her pain. "But I don't have nobody to help me, but you."

"And I can't lose you, now, Money. I can't!" Melissa's voice seized in her throat. "Okay. I'll ask him—"

****

When Melissa finally drummed up the courage later that afternoon, she put a call through to Douglas' office. "Hi, Charlotte, is Douglas in?" She strained to keep her voice from quivering.

"Why, no. Sorry, Mrs. Grand." Charlotte hesitated. "He's out for the rest of the afternoon.

"Oh, that's right?" Melissa pretended to be in the know. "I forgot. He's meeting with Harry Harp, the guitarist?"

"No." Charlotte slowed, hoping she was doing the right thing. She'd heard the raised voices on Melissa's last day in the office, and it wouldn't be a scene she'd soon forget. Besides, she knew it wasn't healthy to cross her boss. "Mr. Grand is meeting with Willamina Redd on some last minute details—"

"No need to explain." Melissa managed a hoarse chuckle. "Mega-concert rocks; right? They're probably over at the Grand Ole Opry—"

"No, that rehearsal got cancelled," Charlotte said before she thought. "They shifted their meeting to Chez Jacques."

Melissa sucked in a hot breath, remembering it was nearly three years to the day that Douglas had first taken her there on a cool April evening. "But that's our place—"

"And it's a good thing, too." Charlotte clucked cheerfully. "Otherwise, I wouldn't have been able to get dinner reservations at such short notice. You know how booked they always are—"

"Yes." Melissa cut her off in a raspy whisper. "I know."

"Well, because you and Mr. G have A-1 status over there, the maître-d made special arrangements to get them in."

"Oh, I see." Melissa struggled to keep up her charade as she recalled the play-by-play of her first special night with Douglas at Chez Jacques, remembering every intimate detail with crystal clarity. "So…do you know if they plan to go over to the Hotel Carlisle after their meet? Maybe I can catch up with the two of them there."

"No, I don't think so," Charlotte said casually. "But Mr. G does have standing reservations for a suite over there since it's the only five-star, boutique hotel in the heart of downtown." She giggled. "And it just happens to be the favorite watering hole for Country legends, music icons, and the rich and famous. So Mr. G loves to frequent the spot—"

Melissa slammed down the phone. "Money, where are you when I need you?" She cried out over the emptiness of her situation. "How could you get yourself locked up in some God-forsaken jail at a time like this? It's your third strike, you fool, and they're going to put you away for the rest of your life! And I'll be alone…all alone!"

"Douglas is taking Willamina Redd to *our* spot...on *our* night...to *our* hotel." She screamed bitterly. "He's treating her the same way he treated me...and maybe...with the same results. Oh, Money, he's going to dump me for Miss Redd, just like he dumped Wanza for me!" She screeched; all of her hopes and dreams dissolving like cotton candy right before her eyes. "And I can't stand it! I cannot stand it! And you're not here!" She picked up her antique Tiffany lamp and flung it at the floor-to-ceiling portrait of her and Douglas sharing a smiling embrace.

"I need you, Money!" Melissa quivered. "Oh, I need you! And all you left behind are some...painkillers!" She wiped her eyes with the backs of her hands and mourned the shards of green, luminescent glass, which had slashed her prized oil canvas from top to bottom. "And, oh—" Her chest heaved in wild desperation. "Oh...how I need my pain killed!"

Barefooted, Melissa crept out onto the front porch and pushed open the secret door in the column to the right of the stairs. She grabbed up a handful of Money's capsules, resealed the plastic bag and carefully replaced it behind the closed door. Pills in hand, she rambled around in the bar fridge until she found an unopened bottle of the finest French champagne. She uncorked it; sat the pills and the chilled bottle on her nightstand; and went into her ornate bathroom to take a hot, steaming bath.

Melissa put on her finest negligee, propped upon her luxurious bed pillows and toasted herself. "This one is to Money," she said and popped the first pill, "the brother that I love dearly who has abandoned me in my darkest hour." She washed the pill down with a slug of champagne straight from the bottle. "This one is to my selfish Mother and Daddy...and all their cheating and their lies." She spouted, followed by another pill and another long draw on the champagne bottle. "This next one is to my worm of a husband, Douglas Grand, who never has time for me, who lies to me, and who cannot give me the baby he knows I want so desperately…and didn't have the common decency to tell me!" Her wide-eyed rage burned red hot. "But he'll change his tune when he finally comes home and sees how miserable he's made me. And then…he'll look at me, again…the same way he's looking at Willamina Redd, right this minute." She wailed bitterly and followed it by another pill and another long swig. "And this one," she said, screaming at the top of her lungs, "is to you, Miss Willamina Redd, who's sitting in the exact same seat I sat in three years ago…and you're no better than me…tsk-tsk-tsk…consorting with a married man!" She wobbled and took another pill and another pull from the bottle. "Hey, now, isn't this some twisted fate?" She pulled her fine brocade satin coverlet up to her neck. "And if tradition holds true to form, I guess Miss Redd is being whisked off to the Hotel Carlisle to screw my husband…just like I screwed Wanza's. Ha-Ha-Ha!" Melissa's laughter broke down into loud, gut-wrenching sobs. She swallowed the remaining pills and finished off the bottle.

CHAPTER 31
Gold Wash

Meanwhile, three streets over, Douglas Grand was giving Willamina Redd the star treatment. "I'm so glad you had time to dine with me this evening," Douglas said, as he escorted Miss Redd to the chauffeur-driven Rolls Royce limo that he'd arranged to be parked in her expansive, circular driveway—the pride of Peacock Place. "You are the new Grammy-winning Queen of Country; you've introduced me to this fabulous new world; we are about to take the music industry by storm; and I am forever in your debt." He gave her a sweeping, gallant bow. He was decked out in a dashing, gray tailored suit that set-off all his manly features to their best advantage.

"Wow!" Willamina giggled as she stepped out and locked her front door on the cool April evening in Nashville. "If you'd let me know I'd be riding in luxury," she said with her famous southwest twang, "I'd a put my fancy, new boots on." She had on an elaborate pair of eel-skin boots and a black pant suit of the finest kid leather and a ruby-red blouse, which sparkled against her fair skin and set her red hair to blazing.

"You're kidding, right?" Douglas eyed her up and down as he swung open the rear door of the limo to allow her to enter. "You look absolutely amazing."

"Well, thank you, kind sir." Willamina tossed back her pretty redhead. "I appreciate the compliment."

When she'd settled in, Douglas presented her with a bouquet of fresh blue bonnets, which had as its center, one perfect yellow rose. "Had them flown in today from Texas." His voice lowered to a deep drum roll. "Only the best for the best."

"Oh, my goodness." Willamina gasped, not knowing quite what to make of Douglas' chivalrous overtures. But she smiled sweetly and said, "They're beautiful. Thank you."

"Champagne?"

"No." Willamina smiled as she took a look at the chilled bottle of Dom Pérignon. "Don't drink; hinders my voice."

"Then I'll have one for the both of us." Douglas popped the cork. "I feel like celebrating. My mega concert is only three weeks away, and all systems are raring to go!"

"So you got all the media and publicity lined up like you wanted it?" Willamina traced the excitement on his strong, handsome face. "You seemed a bit worried about that last week."

"All done...and none too soon." Douglas raved. "Mark my words. We're going to set this town, this nation, this universe on its ear. We're going to set a new, platinum standard for live concert performances!"

When they arrived at Chez Jacques, Jean-Claude, the maître de, greeted Douglas like they were old friends. He took special care to ensure that he and his beautiful guest were seated at his favorite corner table, drenched in flickering candlelight.

"Thanks, Jean-Claude. I know this was short notice." Douglas said when they were ushered to their table. He slipped him a crisp, one-hundred-dollar bill for his troubles.

"This is lovely," Willamina said; her smile as bright as the candlelight.

"I thought you would like it." Douglas' raspy voice deepened. "It's one of my favorite places in the city."

"So is there some additional business we need to discuss?" Willamina offered him a sweet smile after the white-gloved waiter came and went.

"No." Douglas' eyes drank her in like the red wine in his glass. "Tonight," he said, his voice rumbling like the downbeat of distant thunder, "is a night for our own, personal pleasure—"

"Oh." Willamina blushed down to her neck.

"I've been wanting to get you alone like this for some time." Douglas commenced his rap. "So I can tell you what a fine woman I think you are. In fact, you're the lady I've been looking for all my life."

Willamina was at a loss for words, so she said nothing.

"Is your steak properly prepared?" Douglas asked. "Because if it's not, Jean-Claude would be happy to make it right—"

"No." Willamina stopped him. "My steak is excellent." She lowered her beautiful blue eyes and locked them on his wide, platinum wedding band.

"Then what's wrong?" Douglas reached across the table and took her soft, white hand into his. "Do I make you feel uncomfortable?"

"You are a very attractive man, Douglas Grand." Willamina slowly withdrew her hands and sat them in her lap. "But I know your wife, and I'm a member of your church."

"You know both my wives, but what's that got to do with it?" Douglas grumbled.

"I think you know." Willamina blushed, and the candlelight flickered in her luminous blue eyes.

"But you don't understand." Douglas' voice strummed rich and deep like the lower registers on an accomplished bass guitar. "I have real, deep feelings for you, Willa—"

"Feelings come and feelings go," Willamina said quietly."

"But I can prove it to you." Douglas' smoky voice smoldered, thick with desire. "Let me prove it to you…get to know me better—"

"Jesus." Willamina breathed and closed her eyes on the tempting appeal of Douglas' attractive face and virile, sexy body—a body she'd love to ravage under different circumstances. *What woman*

166

doesn't want to hear she's irresistible to a very desirable man? And that voice of his, boy-howdy! "But Jesus says I cannot cross that line," Willamina said, making every effort to temper her voice so that her conflicting emotions wouldn't give her away. "So I can't cross that line—"

"Are you saying you'd consider it if I got rid of—"

"No." Willamina's voice firmed. "I wouldn't have anything to do with a man who left his wife on my account—"

"But Willamina, you get me—my life, my ambition, my world. We share so much in common, and we could share so much more." Douglas' raspy voice rumbled like thick logs on a roaring fire. "Baby, you complete me—"

"But you're a married man, Douglas. That's an established fact." Willamina rebutted, barely able to deny her body's response to this man's charms. "And *we* are never gonna happen—not now, not ever." *Flee! Flee*! She stood and dropped her napkin into her half-eaten plate.

"Wait." Douglas pleaded. "Does this mean you're backing out of the concert, too?"

"Not on your life, Cowboy." Willamina casually flipped back her flowing red hair, even though her knees were weak from going three-rounds of temptation with this very seductive man. Not wanting Douglas to see his effect on her, she braced herself against the back of her chair and said smoothly, "You're way too good at what you do for me to walk away from your talent. I really do need you—"

"Then get to know me better—"

"But—" Willamina rustled up a brave smile and set her index finger against her rosy lips to stave off his pleas. "Let's just keep it strictly professional from here on out, okay? See you at rehearsals next week." And without waiting for Douglas to weaken her resolve, Willamina twirled on her heels and marched over to the maître d' to order a cab. Maybe, she'd be able to make it in time for Wanza's big night at True Vine.

Crushed, Douglas sat at his table for a long while, nursing his after dinner liqueur. *Can't go home...not to Melissa and all her hysterics.* He mulled over his options. *Guess I'll just bed down at the Hotel Carlisle tonight...alone.* His lips curled into a wicked smile. *But Miss Redd...did I detect a little chink in your armor? I've got yo' Cowboy, alright! And have no fear, Little Lady, I'm not done with you yet...not by a long shot.*

CHAPTER 32
Pure Gold

Meanwhile, on this eventful April evening, Wanza was making her acceptance speech as the newly-installed director of the latest, cutting-edge ministry at True Vine. The auditorium was packed with young, single mothers. Many of the social service agencies were represented and they'd made their clients' attendance mandatory. Mrs. Lawson, Director of the Women's Services Center, was perched front row and center. Willamina Redd was at her elbow. The lights were bright and decorations lovely, despite the *tooty-lips* and the *I-ain't-trying-to-hear-that* expressions that were weighing heavily on the room.

"Good evening. My name is Wanza Johnson-Grand. And I've been dipped in the fire." She proclaimed shakily amidst a wash of doubtful eyes. "I've been poor; and I've been rich. I've been married; and I've been divorced. I've been cheated on; and I've been dumped. I've been lied to; and I've been mistreated. And, now, I'm a single mother raising two young boys." Wanza raised stoic eyes and connected with her audience. "And like many of you in this room tonight, I used to think the world owed me something…for how badly I'd been treated. I was looking at what others had, and I did not." Her voice spiked. "And I wanted somebody to pay!"

With that, the audience began to sit up and take better notice of this trim, fit beauty who was somehow speaking their language. But little did they know, having subscribed to the mantra that *nothing good ever comes easy*, Wanza had submitted herself to a rigorous discipline of diet and exercise. And being able to fit into the same sized-14, cream-colored silk suit tonight, which she'd married Douglas in 17 years earlier, was her own, sweet reward.

"And so." Wanza continued, feeling the boldness of her convictions starting to stir in her soul. "You sit here tonight thinking it's your right to game the system—do nothing, give nothing, and live on other people's handouts and their choices for your life—because they owe you; right?" Her eyes scoured the room. "But no matter how clever and tricky you think yourself to be, there just never seems to be enough. Am I right?" She paused to the gasps of women feeling like they were being outed in public by one of their own. "You see, I know you," Wanza said bluntly. "I was you. And, like some of you, I was so angry and bitter and toxic…and despite all of the resources at my disposal, I was mean and unhappy and going nowhere fast…until I met Jesus."

Wanza resituated herself at the podium, feeling the fire of passion burning in her chest where anger had once ruled. "And then one day I realized…Lord, this situation is just what you want for me…so You can show me that You alone are able to meet all my needs…and I can share what you've done for me with the rest of the world." She smiled sweetly. "And, now, I thank Him every morning for tearing down my kingdom of bitterness, disappointment, and hatred, so He can build up His kingdom of faith, and hope, and love inside me."

Wanza batted back her tears. "So I stand here tonight and admit to you—I've been dipped in the fire—ooo-wee, yes, Lord!" She grinned. "But the very same fire that could've burned me up and taken away my life, God used it to get my attention—*wake me up*—so He could save me and give my life true purpose and meaning. And whatever fire you find yourselves in this evening, ladies, He is willing and able to do the same thing for you…if you'll let Him."

Wanza paused to catch Pastor Meadows' eye before she said, "And we, here, at Dipped in the Fire Ministries—" Pastor Meadows smiled and nodded his approval. And Wanza repeated it more confidently, "And we at Dipped in the Fire Ministries are here to help you and your children on your journey."

"Of course, we're grateful for and will continue to partner with all of the agencies and foundations that provide resources to young women with children who're trying to find their way. But we also realize, without a firm foundation, it won't matter how much stuff and how many resources well-meaning people throw at you; it won't mean a thing. It'll be like tossing it down into a bottomless pit that can never be filled. You'll never have enough." Wanza smiled. "But with a firm foundation of faith in Jesus Christ, you can take those same resources you've been given and build a solid life for you and your children."

"And if you can find in yourself to say, like I did, 'Yes, I grew up hard, but I want better for me and my kids.'" Wanza looked away from her notes and poured out her heart to her audience. "And if that's what you really want—if that's your heart's desire—it will be my joy—" She cast a soft gaze on Pastor Meadows, Candi Meadows, and Y. "It will be our joy to introduce you to our Lord and Saviour, who sees us dipped in the fire of our circumstances—and no matter how hot they may be—He has the awesome power to bring us up out of them…as pure gold!"

Wanza stopped abruptly, just short of tears. Her heart was humbled to breaking by the very warm and very unexpected standing ovation that she received.

EPILOGUE
Strike Gold

Douglas Grand was the first to arrive into the empty parking lot at True Vine Ministries, Inc. on that crisp, fall morning in October. He wanted to dress for his wedding at the church rather than risk any wrinkles in his gray tuxedo with tails, which he'd had tailor-made for the special occasion. When he stepped out of his custom, baby-blue Bentley, Money Mann stepped out of the shadows.

"What-the-What!" Douglas fumbled. "What're you doing here? I thought you were on your third strike…in jail for the rest of your miserable life," he said with a swagger.

"Naw." Money rolled his toothpick between clenched teeth. "That's all just a vicious rumor, Man. I didn't do no murder. It was a case of mistaken identity."

"So they let you off, huh?" Douglas smirked. "But they wouldn't let you out for Melissa's funeral."

"Naw, they just couldn't make that happen…seeing as how you threw Missy in the ground so fast." Money shrugged coolly. "Guess you didn't wanna mess up your mega concert schedule, huh?"

"Well, the show must go on, as they say." Douglas smiled, showing off his perfect white teeth.

"Yeah, and I see you're driving a Bentley, now, since your mega concert took the world by storm." Money drawled in his familiar, cool style. "What that net you, Man—$20 million; $50 million—"

"Well, I did alright." Douglas swayed with a little peacock shuffle. "But what're you doing here?"

"Who? Me?" Money eyed him and shrugged. "Saw your wedding announcement in the newspaper—flashy spread for a flashy guy." He grinned and produced a .38 caliber Smith & Wesson pistol from under his leather jacket. "So I'm here to kill you…for killing my sister…and before you get a chance to mess up another young woman's life—"

"But-but…I didn't kill your sister." Douglas' designer suit bag dropped down onto the gritty pavement. "I wasn't even home the night she died—"

"Yeah." Money trained his gun squarely at Douglas' head. "That's what the coroner tells me. And he also tells me that Missy might've survived the overdose if somebody had o' found her in time. But nooo, you were off romancing Willamina Redd while my po' sister was snatching for her last breath—"

"Not so!" Douglas' words trembled with a mixture of fear and anger. "I never had…relations…with Willamina while Melissa was still alive. Never!"

Money used the gun barrel to tilt back his stingy-brimmed hat with a chuckle. "So…she wouldn't have you, huh?" He sneered. "Miss Redd had the good sense to turn you down 'cause she knew you was a married man?"

"But I—"

"Did you know those capsules Missy took were filled with A-grade, un-cut heroin—"

"Ye-s." Douglas fidgeted nervously. "The coroner told me. But they never found out how Melissa got them." His voice shrilled into high gear. "They weren't mine. I swear. I'd never bring drugs into my home—"

"Naw." Money's voice dropped, heavy with remorse. "They were mine." He admitted. "I told Missy I'd leave my stash in our secret spot, so the cops wouldn't find it on me. She thought they were just…painkillers—"

"You, see! You, see!" Douglas sniveled in his own defense. "It's not my fault. Melissa wasn't trying to kill herself! She wasn't even trying—"

"But she *was* trying to get your attention—"

"But she'd still be alive today…if it had been just painkillers—"

"You see, this was gonna be my last big score, Man." Money produced the baggie containing the rest of his stash with his non-gun-toting hand. "I wanted to stand on my own two feet…leave that life behind me. I wanted to stop sticking my hand into Melissa's pocket and your bank account. This one last transaction was gonna net a hundred grand on my end…and a million on the street." He let the drug capsules spill out onto the concrete. "But instead, they cost my sister her life—"

"See! See!" Douglas seized upon the opportunity to shift the blame. "I told you. It wasn't me. I didn't have anything to do with your sister's death—"

"Shut your pie-hole!" Money raged. "You had everything to do with it! You're the reason she took the pills in the first place! It was a cry for help, Man! Don't you see?" The loaded pistol shook wildly in Money's hand. "You tormented my sister from morning to night. You knew she wanted a baby…but you had your twinkie clipped, and you didn't even bother to tell her. You knew she wasn't the one to work with your hoodlum clients…but you pushed her into it anyway. You knew she wanted your love more than life itself…but you ignored her. You backed her into a corner—" Money's voice broke like shards of glass as his mind scrolled back to the cold form he'd found sprawled out on their kitchen floor so many years before. "Just like…our Daddy—"

"But I didn't know—"

"You knew!" Money roared in a guttural growl. "You make it your business to know…the strengths and weaknesses of everybody in your circle…and then you find a way to exploit every one of them to your own advantage. You're a vicious dog, Douglas Grand!" Money pulled back the hammer and cocked his gun. "And I'm gonna put you outta your misery—"

"No!" Douglas rolled into a whimpering ball—no flash, no dash, not this time—just raw, stinking fear. "No...please...please!" Douglas groveled down to his knees. "You're right. I did it. I did everything you said...but please...please...don't kill me!"

"I sat in that jail cell, Doug, long enough to figure out the method to your madness." Money's voice shrilled. "When you were trying to get next to the bluesmen in this town, you used a *round-the-way* girl like Wanza 'cause she could talk-the-talk and walk-the-walk and make you look legit—with your fake behind." The pistol trembled in Money's hand. "And when you wanted to move up to high society, you picked Missy 'cause she was gorgeous, and smart, and polished and made you look good—with your fake behind. And now that you've got big-bank, you think a white girl can take you places a black girl can't, so you pick pretty, rich, rising star, Miss Redd—"

"That's not—"

"You married Missy six months after you got rid of Wanza. And, now, you're marrying Miss Redd six months after you got rid of Missy. You must be setting some kind o' record, Man." Money sneered. "And how must po' Miss Wanza and her boys be feeling 'bout all yo' wild shenanigans—"

"Wanza and Willamina...they've made their peace. I swear!" Douglas sniveled. And I really do love—"

"Save it!" Money shook his pistol in Douglas' face. "You don't love nobody, but yourself. You don't want a wife; you want an opportunity—an opportunity to move up another rung on yo' self-made ladder to success. You're the worst kind o' man, Doug— you're a sadistic predator—a straight-up user—and these po' women are merely collateral damage in yo' own sick game." Money was trembling with anger, now, and the pistol was wavering dangerously in his hand as he battled to hold back his tears. "But if you didn't want my sister, Man," he said, sniveling like a damaged child, "why...why didn't you just let her go? Why didn't you just let her go, Man? Let her go!"

"But Money—"

"Don't say my name!" Money aimed the pistol a straight shot to Douglas' nose. "Missy gave me that name—"

"Okay-Okay!" Douglas cowered down under his hands and lost control of his bladder. "I'll give you anything...anything you want...you name it...just don't shoot me...don't shoot me... please...don't shoot me!"

Money drew in a sharp breath that made a whistling sound. He snapped down on his toothpick and took a swift step backwards. He used the heel of his shoe to grind the drugs into the concrete. He stretched out his bad knee and stuffed the empty baggie back into his pocket. "Get up!" Money demanded, looking down at Douglas' soiled condition. "Go change your pants, D-o-u-g." He jeered out his name. "You ain't gonna die here today." He released the hammer and un-cocked his pistol. "At least not by my hands. But I hope Miss Redd gets so sick o' yo' mess, she stabs you with a dull kitchen knife." Money clucked wickedly. "The woman is from *Cut-n-Shoot*, Texas, you know."

"Thanks, Man! Thanks!" Douglas began to breathe, again. He swept up his precious suit bag and slunk toward the church as more cars began to roll into the parking lot. "And you don't have to worry." He looked back over his shoulder at Money. "I won't tell. I won't tell a soul—"

"True dat!" Money replaced his pistol in the back of his waistband and covered it over with his jacket. "'Cause you don't wanna tangle with me...not ever, again." He turned to walk away as sirens could be heard screaming in the distance. "You go on in that church...you marry po' Miss Redd...mess up her life, too." Money squeezed down his stingy-brimmed hat with both of his tattooed hands. "When Missy was living, I tried to keep the *Mann-mystique*

176

alive...protect her from the pain of this world. I thought it was my duty...no matter what it cost me. But now...I'm leaving you devilish church folk behind...and demon rum, too." He gave his nose a solid swipe. "And I'm gonna do what Mother Whatnot told me to do a long time ago." Money twirled his toothpick like a twizzle stick as he strolled away. "I'm gonna get to know Jesus...for myself."

****

"For he that soweth to his flesh shall of the flesh reap corruption;
but he that soweth to the Spirit shall of the Spirit reap life everlasting."
Galatians 6:8

Other Books by the Author
JEANETTA BRITT

Exciting Novels

Living in the Seventh Day (ISBN 978-0-6923005-0-3)

W.O.O.F. (Women of Overcoming Faith) (ISBN 978-0-9712363-8-7)

Empty Envelope (ISBN 978-0-9712363-5-6)

The Lottie Series:

    Pickin' Ground (Book 1)   (ISBN 0-9712363-3-x)

    In Due Season (Book 2)   (ISBN 0-9712363-4-8)

    Lottie (Book 3)   (ISBN 0-9712363-6-4)

[E-Books are also available for Kindle and Nook.]

Inspiring Poetry

Flittin' & Flyin' (ISBN 978-0-9712363-9-4)

Under the Influence--Spoken Praise (ISBN 0-9712363-7-2)

The Trilogy:

    Poems from the Fast   (ISBN 0-9712363-0-5)

    Reunion   (ISBN 0-9712363-1-3)

    Third Ear   (ISBN 0-9712363-2-1)

Join Jeanetta online:

www.jbrittbooks.com

www.Facebook.com/Jeanetta Britt

www.Facebok.com/JBrittBooks

www.Twitter.com/@JBrittBooks

www.Amazon.com/Jeanetta Britt

www.bn.com/Jeanetta Britt

ABOUT THE AUTHOR

Jeanetta Britt is a bestselling author who graduated with honors from Fisk University and The University of Michigan. Her passion for writing contemporary Christian Fiction novels—filled with lots of juicy drama and suspense—as well as, Gospel poetry, surfaced in 1996 and has grown steadily since that time. "While being swept up in the story," Jeanetta says, "I want my readers to *feel* the love of Jesus and take refuge in Him, like I did."

After completing a rewarding career in public administration in Dallas, Texas, Jeanetta returned to her native Alabama to write and to live. Her southern roots are reflected in her strong imagery, memorable characters, and delightfully witty storytelling style. She is a sought-after inspirational speaker, by youth and adults alike, with seven novels and five books of poetry to her credit.

Jeanetta is also an avid gardener and community advocate, and she founded Twelve Stones CDC—a non-profit organization that operates two community gardens in rural Alabama. "We provide free, fresh food for our community and an opportunity for our youth and senior citizens to form vital intergenerational connections, and to get some free exercise, companionship and sunshine, too," she says. "No rules—just love!"